A. N. Homer

The Woman he loved

Vol. I

A. N. Homer

The Woman he loved
Vol. I

ISBN/EAN: 9783337053178

Printed in Europe, USA, Canada, Australia, Japan

Cover: Foto ©Andreas Hilbeck / pixelio.de

More available books at **www.hansebooks.com**

THE WOMAN HE LOVED.

A Novel.

BY

A. N. HOMER.

" She was his life,
The ocean to the river of his thoughts,
Which terminated all."

BYRON.

IN THREE VOLUMES.

VOL. I.

London:

F. V. WHITE & CO.,

31, SOUTHAMPTON STREET, STRAND, W.C.

1888.

PRINTED BY
KELLY AND CO., GATE STREET, LINCOLN'S INN FIELDS, W.C.:
AND MIDDLE MILL, KINGSTON-ON-THAMES.

CONTENTS.

THE WOMAN HE LOVED.

THE WOMAN HE LOVED.

CHAPTER I.

IN THE EDEN GARDENS.

THE Indian sun had set and night had shrouded in sultry gloom the splendid capital of the Bengal Presidency. The heavy-winged adjutants were perched, like motionless sable spectres, on every convenient buttress and angle of the grand and stately buildings set apart for the home of the representatives of England's greatness. But no sound issued from the huge precincts of the Viceregal residence; scarce a light illumined the long lines of windows which perforated its frontage. The Viceroy was away at Simla, and for the time being Calcutta was comparatively speaking empty; most of the wealthy inhabitants had gone to the hills in quest of the cooler, more bracing air, not caring to face the fiery glow of the summer sun in the city on the plains. Yet to an unaccustomed eye—to one who did not know the town— the place seemed gay enough. Wandering through the shady groves of the Eden gardens, and listening to the strains of the military band, paced crowds of people, conversing in many languages and dialects and clad in a multiplicity of long, loose-robed, white and parti-coloured Eastern garbs. Outside the gardens, on the Esplanade, numerous well-appointed carriages moved slowly up and down, followed closely by the Hindu servants busied in flicking from the horses' flanks those pests to Anglo-Indian life, the swarming myriads of mosquitoes. Many a half-stifled curse found vent in Hindoostanee as a two-horsed gharry drove recklessly in and out amidst the long lines of vehicles, tenanted by three or four jolly-looking midshipmen, scorning music for that evening at least, and bent upon going for a spree.

Choked with laughter, and heedless of care as they were of life and limb, they went their way regardless of the scowling visages of the red-turbaned chokedars, dressed in their white uniforms and armed with truncheons like European police.

Not a stone's-throw from the lively, fashionable promenade were moored long lines of merchant vessels—clipper ships side by side with clumsy-looking wooden hulks of every conceivable rig and possible nationality. Tall, taper spars, mazy networks of rigging, short, thick funnels of steamers from every quarter of the globe, were reflected in the deep, rapid current of the Hooghly. Under the glare of the gas-lamps, on the closely-shaven turf, near the band-stand, a young fellow stood unattended. To judge him by his figure—which was, if anything, over six feet—he had reached manhood, for he was firmly set up and, though thin, his broad, square shoulders and deep chest showed signs of great strength. But as he turned, and peered anxiously at the moving mass of people, as if in quest of some one, the light shone on an almost boyish face. The features many would have considered as not strictly handsome. Yet, had they looked again, they would have been forced to admit that truth and a brave, open-hearted, loving candour beamed in his dark-blue eyes. That there was no lack of decision to be traced in his well-cut mouth and strongly-moulded chin. They would have decided, had they been physiognomists, that the face before them belonged to one capable of doing and daring much, of loving long and deeply, yet haughty and passionate withal.

"Confound him! why there he is, after having kept me waiting full half an hour," he muttered, as his scrutiny seemed to have been rewarded by a sight of the man he sought. Very nearly knocking over an old, bent-backed, wrinkled-visaged Parsee in his sudden effort to overtake his friend, he called out:

"Geoffrey! Carelesse! Where the deuce are you off to?"

"Oh, there you are. Just looking for you, Clarencourt."

"Time you were," responded Clarencourt. "You can't keep an appointment, Geoffrey, my boy. Never could, and never will, eh? No matter; tell me all about yourself. We hadn't a moment, you know, last night. But who would have thought of meeting you, and out here, too, in the 'City of Palaces!'—the first man to tumble across to be Geoffrey Carelesse, my old chum and school companion! Well, it is odd."

Those words, spoken lightly by Gerard Clarencourt, recalled much. He was an only child; his father having died when he was quite a boy. And his mind at that moment, as he recollected the face of Carelesse as he had last seen it, by a rapid current of thought brought back to him his past, remembrance of his mother, of his home in southern Devon, where she lived and where he had been born —the home of his childhood. His eyes filled with a soft, gentle light as he bent them upon his friend of bygone years, and said:

"What news of yourself, Carelesse? Has the world treated you well? I recollect the wish of your heart was to enter the army."

"And it has been fulfilled. I contrived, I never quite knew how, to squeeze through the examinations; not with any great credit, nevertheless sufficiently well to pass, but only at my last shot. What I should have done had I failed I don't know: enlisted in the Cape Mounted, or bought a couple of flannel shirts and a pickaxe and gone out to the diggings. But here I am, sound, wind, limb and eyesight, and better than all, gazetted to the 10th Regiment of the Line. You see, I am not like you, Gerard, with plenty of the needful. The coin my old uncle sees fit to send me is about enough to keep me in cigars. But to inquisitive mammas I repeat the oft-told tale that I have prospects; and by good luck I hope to get on."

Geoffrey Carelesse, in height, build, appearance, in short, everything, was just the very reverse to Clarencourt, who was several inches the taller of the two. But though certainly not good-looking, and possessed of short - cropped, decidedly carroty - coloured hair, and even a nose which could not be called by any other name than a snub, he looked smart and soldierly in his undress uniform, and no one could have mistaken him for anything but a gentleman. But what told most in his favour was that, as a rule, he was a general favourite with the women, and one must admit that sometimes they are a trifle eccentric in their tastes.

"By the way, Clarencourt, I must offer you a score of apologies for not inquiring sooner; but how is your mother, or rather how was she when you heard last?"

A shade of annoyance passed over Clarencourt's face, like a cloud, which melted next instant into something approaching an expression of sorrow. For a moment he seemed as if about to confide some secret trouble to his friend, but the look fled and left him cold and calm, almost stern, as he drew himself up stiffly and said :

"I thank you, Carelesse ; when last I heard from her she was well."

He did not add what was the truth, that he had received no communication from her as yet. And a mail had come in since he arrived.

"But you ; why have I had no word for all these months?" continued Clarencourt.

"Well, to tell you the truth, old boy, I am the very deuce at writing. Can't bear it. Simply detestable. No end of people are down on me—say I'm the worst correspondent living, and all that sort of thing. I suppose I am, but I can't help it."

"Yes, I know it is one of your pet aversions, but had half hoped you would make an exception in my favour and drop me a line sometimes for the sake of past days."

"And so I will, old boy; at least I will try to."

"Oh, don't trouble, that is unless you really care; but friends, worthy of the

name, are few and far between," added
Clarencourt with a touch of sadness in the
rich mellow tones of his voice.

"Now, Clarencourt, you are getting crusty.
You don't mean to tell me that already you
have found the world hollow and heartless."

"I won't say that; perhaps it would be
too sweeping an assertion for one with so
poor an experience as myself to make—but
cold, yes."

"Well, there is one thing for which you
can thank your lucky stars, and that is
that you can afford to snap your fingers in
the face of what you term the world in
general. For you have that which it wor-
ships. That which is potent and powerful
enough now-a days to bring it at your will
grovelling like a beaten cur, to your feet.
You have gold."

"And I would exchange the little I
possess, gladly, for—but pshaw! Why, Pat,
what fools we are! Just fancy you and I
moralizing. It is too absurd. Let us change
the subject."

"Well, you have not told me yet what has brought you out here."

"The wish to travel, to see new sights and scenes—fresh faces. Nothing more."

"Why, Clarencourt, you speak as a man might, were he a score of years your senior. Time enough for you to get grumpy when another half century has passed."

"Ah, well, that is as it may be, but, Carelesse, tell me, who is that?"

"Where, man, whom do you mean? It is like looking for a needle in a hay-stack."

"There, straight in front of us; next to that tall chap with the huge turban."

"By Jove, deuced lucky you spotted her. It is easy to tell that you are a stranger here. Not to know Ada Devereaux. The prettiest woman in Calcutta. And, egad, if that isn't old Steele, our colonel, with her, too. He is always dancing attendance. It is about time he left the women alone."

"You know her?" inquired Clarencourt, eagerly.

"Rather," replied Carelesse gaily. And

then in an undertone to himself he muttered, " Pity I ever did, though. But why
do you ask ? " he continued, addressing
Clarencourt.

" Because I should like to know her too.
Introduce me, will you ? " The request was
spoken quietly enough, but in a low determined tone which to Carclesse's ear sounded
very like a command. And there was a
haughty and imperious ring in Clarencourt's
voice as he made it, which fairly threw the
other off his guard.

" Oh, certainly, if you wish it," he replied,
but lightly as he spoke, the words had barely
left his lips before he repented of having said
them.

" Thanks."

" You shall talk to Steele too. Come
along." In another moment they had
threaded their way through the crush and
the magic words of introduction had been
spoken. Clarencourt never heard them—in
after years never even remembered anything
that he had said during the remainder of the

evening. For an instant, so long as he could without appearing rude, he looked upon the face of the lady before him. He could see that she was beautiful, even in that dim and uncertain light, for they stood in shadow. But it was not her good looks which dazzled him, and seemed to chain him spell-bound for those brief seconds. It was the expression in her eyes as they met his, and then dropped before his steady glance. He was only recalled to himself by hearing her address him:

" So glad to meet you, Mr. Clarencourt. You are a stranger here, I think, for I do not remember having seen you before."

" Yes.   I only landed three days ago."

" And you like Calcutta ? "

" So far, immensely."

" Ah, wait till you know it as well as I do. You will wish yourself back in the old country."

" Why ? Do you ? "

" Yes—at least, sometimes. But tell me, Mr. Clarencourt. Did you come straight out here from England ? "

"Yes; I left Southampton on the third of last month."

"In what line?"

"By one of the P. & O. steamers."

"Ah. I came by the British India. Colonel Devereaux, my husband, preferred them to any other boats." Gerard Clarencourt gasped. The woman at his side married! Could it be possible? Somehow the thought had not entered his head.

"I—I had no idea you were——"

"Married, you would say. Then you did not catch my name."

"No, pardon me, I failed to."

"Oh, it is of no consequence. I am sure I seldom do know who I am talking to at first But yours is a striking one. Devereaux is mine."

"And Colonel Devereaux—he is——"

"Dead," interrupted Mrs. Devereaux softly. There was an awkward pause and Clarencourt felt that he had unwittingly blundered, perhaps through his own clumsiness probed a hidden wound. But somehow, for the life of him he could not tell why, he felt relieved. And yet, had he vexed her? was she offended? They had wandered away to some distance from the band and the groups of promenaders, and were almost alone. The tiny miniature lake, round which grew clumps of cocoa-nut palms, tree ferns, and the long pointed leaves of the banana, lay before them at their very feet. And the high pointed roof of a pretty Burmese pagoda rose amidst the masses of foliage. He could not speak first. The calm peaceful stillness soothed his overheated fancy. But in another moment he knew that all his fears of having given offence were wholly groundless.

"Yes," she murmured gently; "I am all alone now." The rich full tones of her voice were full of pathos; at least so thought Gerard Clarencourt. Again he met her gaze and felt that look thrill strangely through every nerve of his body. Ah! look again, Gerard Clarencourt; look again, and if you could read through and sift feminine arts and wiles, you would learn that before you stands a woman of the world, a finished coquette; heartless, but a perfect actress and mistress of the game she knows best and has studied most: to break men's hearts. The next instant she had turned and discovered that they were quite alone.

"Why, where are Mr. Carelesse and Colonel Steele? They must have missed us somehow. Let us return. It is late and they are positively playing 'God Save the Queen.' Those men handle their instruments exquisitely. Will you find my carriage, Mr. Clarencourt?"

Clarencourt expressed his willingness and pleasure to execute the task in well chosen language. And in a few minutes more they were before the entrance to the Esplanade. Mrs. Devereaux's open barouche was easily found. The liveried servants lowered the steps, and before he could well realize it, she had seated herself.

"Mr. Clarencourt, you will come and dine with me? Where are you living?"

"At the Great Eastern."

"Ah, close to my house. I shall send you

a card and Mr. Carelesse too. So delighted to
see you. Good-bye." In another instant the
well-gloved hand was withdrawn, and Gerard
Clarencourt had raised his hat and watched
the cloud of dust which hid from his sight
this woman in whom, spite of himself, he felt
already a strange interest.

CHAPTER II.

THE BUNGALOW.

As Gerard Clarencourt had said, he had taken up his quarters at the Great Eastern Hotel, and his rooms there were as comfortable as apartments in hotels generally are, and like them in most respects. He did not occupy a sitting-room as he preferred to breakfast in the coffee-room and dine at the *table-d'hôte*, so he merely occupied his own particular sanctum, near which his servant was accommodated, for he had left England with his valet. At first he had been greatly averse to this arrangement, as he thought it would be a useless expense as well as a great nuisance, and for many reasons he would far rather have travelled alone. But Mrs. Clarencourt had expressed her wish on the subject in haughty measured tones, and Gerard had

2

given way with a good grace because she was his mother. Towards the last, when all the arrangements had been completed, and even his sticks and a gun-case strapped up and labelled for Calcutta, Gerard had glanced at his watch and found that he had not too much time to catch the train. It had been in those last few minutes that he had looked and longed in vain for that love which was his due and which he had every right to expect from his mother. And then, too, it had been that more keenly than ever he had realized what a terrible loss he had sustained when the breath had vanished from the body of the man who had loved him so fondly, and he had looked his last on the dead, passionate face, with its grand intellectual forehead and noble features ivory in whiteness, when it had once and for all felt the cold touch of God's angel and crossed to the other side. Yes, Gerard Clarencourt had bowed like a bruised wind-blown reed before the terrible blow, and had realized bitterly the significance of the fact that *never again, never*, on this side the gloomy valley which lay between them now, should he feel the caress of that hand, loving and gentle as a woman's, or the touch of those kindly lips which had pressed his infant brow with many a good-night kiss and whispered blessing. And so he had looked for love from his mother and found a voice which chilled him. Still he had striven to win her affection, but in vain. And if he had ever needed proof that he had it not, he had received it in that farewell kiss with which she had brushed his forehead lightly as though he had been leaving her but for a day. And yet she could not tell when she gave it that it was not the last. He had forced back the tears of love and wounded pride that *she* might not see his weakness, and had left the house with the dull leaden feeling at his heart, the choking sensation in his throat which *would* come, because he knew now that none loved him. Thus he had gone forth determined to trouble her but little with his presence who could treat him so lightly.

The Great Eastern was tolerably full, and

being far and away the busiest and most
fashionable house of its kind in Calcutta the
noise and bustle in the corridors might well
have awakened Gerard, but despite that and
the fact that Wilson, his man, had been into his
room more than once, he slumbered soundly.
Fearing that perhaps he was not well at
length Wilson made bold to address him :

" Mr. Gerard." He had learnt no other name,
as an old, tried servant of his father's, who
had remembered him ever since he was big
enough to toddle, and taught him how to clear
his first fence. " Mr. Gerard," he repeated,
shaking him gently by the shoulder ; " it is
getting late, sir, and I was thinking that
may be you might wish to be up."

Gerard stirred, shook himself and woke.

" Quite right, Wilson, but what is the
time ? "

" Well, it's near nine o'clock, sir, and the
folks here do seem to be about terrible early ;
no end of 'em out for a ride long ago ; but it's
awful hot, sir, already, and the mosquitoes do
worry one so."

" Haven't troubled me much yet."

" Can that be so, sir? They didn't bite me much aboard ship; but here they just settles upon one with their nasty *pings*, and as persistent as if they meant to chaw one up."

" Sorry for that, Wilson, but you'll get used to them. Bring me some chocolate and see about my breakfast; you know what to order, and tell them to have it ready at ten o'clock sharp."

Wilson drew himself up as stiff as a poker. His regard for his young master approached a sort of blind worship, but he never presumed. If he chose to address him he was gratified, but he knew his place.

" Yes, sir," he said briefly, and left the room. As Clarencourt awoke that morning he became oddly impressed with the idea that his life had undergone some change within the last forty-eight hours. The thought had forced itself upon his fancy, and he had not tried to root it out, or to ask himself the reason for its existence. He

cared not, he only felt that it was there.
Since he had arrived in Calcutta he knew
himself to be a different man. Before then
he had taken all things as a matter of
course; he had no trouble, save one, and
that was not ever present to him. He
forgot. To a certain extent he enjoyed
himself, and any excitement which came
in his way he entered into with a fair
amount of zest, but nothing had *specially*
crossed the monotonous current of his
young life to divert it from its ordinary
course, or the well-worn channels in which it
had run in his every day existence, far away
in his pleasant Devonshire home. No place
on earth could have been like it to him
through the innocent years of his life. But
it had lacked that which he had needed
most, *love*, and the charm had been broken.
Roused from his reverie by the entrance of
Wilson carrying his chocolate and a couple
of letters, which had been brought up from
the post-office where he had directed them
to be sent on leaving England, he took

them from his hands, emptied the contents of the cup and then broke the seals. Both bore the London post-mark. The first, he saw at a glance, was from the family solicitor, and was purely relating to business matters; but the other attracted his attention more closely, and was penned in a slight though firm girlish hand, and ran as follows :—

"DEAR GERARD,

"You see I am going to keep my word, and write, though I feel sure you never expected me to do so. We have been in town for the the last few weeks, and I am longing to return to Sidcombe. Mother tells me that I am quite different to girls of my own age, as above all things I ought to care for concerts and theatres and all the other amusements, which are certainly legion in this great place. But I don't. I love fine music, but if I must barter all I have left behind in exchange for it, then give me dear old glorious Devon. You will laugh at me, I know. How lonely you must feel, so far away from home. Do tell me when you think of returning. Will it be before Christmas? What wonderful accounts I shall expect to hear about India when I do see you! May you return safely is the wish of

"Your true friend,

"LILIAN FABYN."

"How good and kind of her to remember me! With most, it is out of sight out of mind," he added, remembering the complete silence on the part of his mother. "I believe Lilian is the only friend I have in the world," he continued musingly. "And I would wager anything that she is true." With those brief words he tossed the note aside, but he little knew how near the truth they were when he spoke them so carelessly. "And now for my tub, and then to dress as quickly as possible. Confound it, how late I am!" he said to himself as he heard a clock chiming the half-hour. In a wonderfully short space of time he had completed his toilette, and having finished breakfast strolled out with the intention of going through some of the bazaars. The sun was insufferably hot, and before he had gone far he turned into a tobacconist's store, ostensibly for the purpose of getting a good cheroot, but in reality to escape the blinding glare. He bought and paid for two or three boxes, ordering them to be sent to the hotel. Then, as he was standing on the steps, puffing away at a crooked looking little Burmah, a thought struck him. He would do as he had done yesterday, and to-day he might be more successful. So summoning a gharry he ordered the driver to go through the Circular Road, and on by the best way he could to Fort William. It was past Mrs. Devereaux's house that Gerard wished to drive. He had not seen her since she had pressed his hand, and bid him good-bye outside the Eden gardens. And he had gone there since, and had watched for her carriage midst the moving mass of others, and sought her face and form in vain. She had not been there. Then late in the night he had wandered aimlessly until the moon had risen high, and its pale cold rays had revealed to him a group of jackals, which scudded on only a few score yards ahead of him, scared by the sound of his footfall on the dried-up, sun-scorched herbage as he took his way across the Madhaun back to his hotel in the still hot, sultry night, dejected and cast down, weary and dissatisfied. As he was borne briskly along on the present occasion he puzzled his brains for reasons to account for her silence. "Why had she not appeared again at the band? And what was the reason for not writing? She had said she would, and she had failed to keep her word." Then again the thought occurred to him that *perhaps* there *was* the possibility that he had offended her by his bluntness. The fact was that he was altogether unreasonable. As the four-wheeled gharry bore him abreast of the bungalow which he had learned by cautious inquiry was hers, he anxiously scanned its white front. No, her figure was not to be seen at any of the many windows which nestled under the verandah, half hidden by tall tree ferns, Cape jasmine, clematis with white and purple flowers, creepers, and other tropical foliage. They had passed the building in a moment and he sank back, annoyed, and just the least bit put out with himself for evincing so much interest in one, almost a total stranger to him.

"Perhaps Carelesse can throw some light on the matter ; she may have written to him," he muttered, as he lounged back, and suffered himself to be borne swiftly in the direction of Fort William. At length they turned down on to the Esplanade, and drove along almost abreast of Princeps Ghaut. Before reaching the entrance to the huge and massive piece of engineering skill, so vast in size as to be quite capable of containing all the white population of Calcutta, Clarencourt got out, paid and dismissed the conveyance, and then sought the officers' quarters.

"Can I see Lieutenant Carelesse?" he inquired of the first man he saw.

"Yes, sir; will you please follow me?" returned he. "He is in there, sir," he continued as they arrived before the entrance to a room, which was closed, "Who shall I say, sir?"

"Mr. Clarencourt," answered Gerard.

"Glad to see you, Clarencourt; make yourself comfortable, and try that chair. I had it made especially for myself," said Carelesse, as he entered,

"Thanks, but why did you not look me up as you promised yesterday? I never thought that you would fail to come."

"No, neither did I, my dear fellow, but it was all owing to that old brute Steele. He piled on some extra duties which I had to attend to," replied Carelesse, who in reality was framing a plausible excuse to account for his non-appearance. "Awfully sorry, but could not help it, you see."

"Oh, no! of course you couldn't; but why is he a brute? Not a favourite of yours, eh?"

" As I with him, so he with me," laughed Carelesse.

" Why ? "

" Oh, he's a bully and a martinet combined, arrogant, supercilious and overbearing in the extreme, and except by men of his own grade—the only way by which he judges of an equal, I believe—thoroughly disliked in the service."

" Rather an unpleasant character to be brought into close contact with."

" By Jove, I should think he is ! " answered Carelesse, warming to the subject. " Of course this is *entre nous*, but fellows who have had the ill-luck to have served under him long, tell me that they have tried every possible device to bring him up before a court-martial ; but he has always been able to hold his own and score against them so far. He is too artful by a long chalk ; Garrick of ours simply hates him."

" Who is *he ?* "

" Oh, a capital fellow ; did some plucky things in the last campaign we had against the Afghans. Just got his company—as brave as a lion, my boy—I shall introduce you some time. But now, about yourself? What have you been doing since I saw you?"

"Very little. I haven't even troubled myself to present half-a-dozen letters of introduction to people here."

"Ah, indeed!" said Carelesse, eyeing him jealously, but only for an instant, for he changed his front, and Clarencourt had no chance of observing the look. What he wished to know he intended to discover by judicious means, so as not to betray his own interest in the subject. "Fancy your coming down here on a deuced hot morning like this! mid-day too; why most of us go in for a quiet siesta."

"I drove," replied Clarencourt.

"Of course you did, but what a rude beggar you must think me. Here have I been jawing away, forgetting that you must be as thirsty as a lime-kiln. Help yourself; there's brandy and soda, some claret, and cheroots which I can swear by."

"Thanks," answered Gerard, pouring out a bumper of soda, dashed with cognac, and taking a long deep pull. "I did feel just a shade done up; this heat does try one at first."

"By-the-by, where the deuce did you take yourself off to after I introduced you to Mrs. Devereaux?" asked Geoffrey, coming round to what he was dying to know.

"The very question I was going to ask you. We strolled on, and Mrs. Devereaux happened to glance back, and could discover you nowhere."

"Why, Steele and I were buttonholed by some men, and when we looked round you were gone. Steele was as crusty as they make 'em, and left me in an awful temper. Of course he said nothing, but I could see he was riled at having had his *tête-à-tête* interrupted." What Carelesse did not remark was far more to the point; that *he* had been affected by the same blow, and that a spirit of distrust had found its way into his heart towards his friend, and that had been the reason why he had not kept his appointment and called upon him as he had promised. It may seem odd, but it is nevertheless a fact, that generally speaking two people, more especially men, who are intimate, and who both chance to be attracted by the same woman, seldom succeed in altogether hiding their thoughts from each other; at least, not as a rule, or for long, no matter how reticent they may be. The same instinctive feeling of jealousy which had entered Carelesse's mind had already established itself in Clarencourt's.

"Have you seen her since?" inquired Carelesse, as he singled out a fresh cheroot.

"No, how should I, my dear fellow? Have you?" asked Gerard quietly.

"No, nor heard from her either."

"Why, does she write to you?"

"Oh, only a card sometimes to ask me up to tiffin if we don't happen to meet."

"Then he knows nothing," thought Clarencourt, "and there can be no good in my mentioning to him her remarks to me about dining." The demon of envy possessed him, and so he quietly drew in his horns and said nothing more on the subject.

"Where do you intend to go to after you leave here?" inquired Carelesse.

"Haven't the faintest idea. I may go up country, but am quite undecided as yet."

"Well, you'll mess with us to-night, and then I can introduce you to Garrick and all our fellows."

"Thanks; I rather dread your green-eyed monster of a colonel."

"Oh, you need not mind him; he'll very likely not turn up."

"Thank you all the same, but I think I will hold myself excused, if you will permit me," answered Clarencourt rather stiffly. "I have got no end of letters to write for next mail, but another day I shall be most happy."

"As you wish, of course, my dear fellow. Then when shall I see you again?"

"Come and look me up to-night if you

have nothing better to do, say nine-thirty. We can have a smoke and a chat over old times."

" Very good, I'm your man."

" Until then, *au revoir*."

Clarencourt turned on his heel, and half-an-hour later was back at his hotel, holding in his hand a tiny scented billet-doux. It was brief and precise, so I venture to give it :

"DEAR MR. CLARENCOURT,

"If you can contrive to favour me with the pleasure of your society at dinner to-night (seven-thirty), upon so short a notice, I shall be delighted to see you. Need I add that this is quite a friendly invitation.

"Yours very truly,

" ADA DEVEREAUX.

" Dilnapoor, Calcutta."

What pleasure those few short lines gave him, and how he studied the signature, the bold free hand in which it was written, and re read it again and again before finally consigning it to his breast-pocket! Yes, he should see her once more, and this time not midst the dusk of evening, which had hid her face from him so that the one glimpse he had had of it was due to the fitful uncertain gleam of the lamps, and with all eyes on him. No, now he should look upon her under more favourable circumstances and judge for himself whether his sight had misled him or no. And yet it could not be that he loved her. Their meeting had only extended over the space of, say half-an-hour, and in those few hurried moments, when they had talked on purely conventional subjects, it would have been impossible for him to have formed the slightest estimation of her character. She might be opposed to him in every way; a thousand and one idiosyncrasies of temperament night interpose between them to check the course of love, to nip and shrivel up, before ever it had time to grow into a passion, the feeling, which as yet could only be one of interest, already awakened in him. Had he been ten years

older, and become what is termed a man of
the world, he would have experienced none
of the restless expectancy, and none of the
almost boyish desires which made him long
for the hands of the clock to move a thousand times more swiftly, and caused him to
scan the face of his watch, and think that
time to him had never seemed so utterly and
hopelessly long. No; had he borne the
uneffaceable stamp which marks the man
who has seen much, and the soft, gentle
edges of whose nature have been gradually
rounded off by close and changeful contact
with life's human stream—a contact, moreover, from which it is impossible to escape
without contamination, for though there may
be the good, there certainly is the bad, and
faith and trust in the mass of surging wrest-
ling mortals is not to be brought about by
a thorough knowledge of them—he would
have evinced nothing more than a listless,
well-bred curiosity, prompted probably by
the desire to discover whether this were
not a new snare flung across his path, like

the old ones so terribly fraught with evil, when he had believed them good and pure; so cruelly unworthy when he had placed unhesitatingly his love and honour in their hands, only to have it ruthlessly flung back upon him. It might have been better—nay, it would have been — had Gerard Clarencourt thus lived and learnt before he chanced to meet Ada Devereaux; but no necessity could have existed in that case to write these lines. At length he threw himself on a sofa and read, and so much did the book interest him that he forgot all, even Ada Devereaux. It was typical of his quick, impulsive nature, easily led by a kindly loving word, but as difficult to control or direct by force or brutality. Wilson roused him up at last by abruptly entering to ask if there were any letters to be posted.

"Yes, four; there they are on the table," answered Clarencourt, flinging the novel down and yawning. Then he suddenly recollected his engagement with Carelesse.

What could he do? It would be impossible to see him. There was no likelihood of his returning early enough to keep the appointment. He could not give up his chance of meeting Mrs. Devereaux — that was out of the question. Rapidly the unpleasant position in which he was placed passed through his mind. Then he decided Carelesse must go to the wall. He would write him a polite note, expressing his re gret, and explaining the matter so far as he was able, but he would make no allusion as to where he was going. Wilson could take it down to the barracks. Seating himself at a table, he wrote a few lines of apology, and directed the envelope to Carelesse. Then he rang the bell, which was promptly answered by his servant.

"I want you to give this letter to Lieutenant Carelesse. He is quartered at Fort William. You know your way?"

"Not quite sure, sir, but I can inquire."

" Oh, you cannot make a mistake, any one

will tell you ; see that he gets it as soon as possible."

" Yes, sir."

" And, Wilson ; I may not be in until late ; don't sit up for me."

" Very good, sir," replied the man in so absent a tone that Gerard looked up, and caught a wistful, yearning expression on his kindly, honest face.

" Is there anything that you wished to say to me ? " he asked. Wilson re-entered the room, and closed the door, which he had held ajar, advancing towards his young master with the familiarity of a tried and trusted servant.

" Beggin' your pardon, sir, but have you had any word yet from Clifford's Wood ? I couldn't keep longer from askin' you, Mr. Gerard."

A shadow, which he could not conceal from the piercing eyes of the other, crossed Gerard's face. The inquiry had touched the weak nerve in his nature. Clifford's Wood was the name of his home ; but he recovered himself almost immediately, and said, with a forced smile :

" No, not yet ; probably next mail will bring some news. Now leave me, Wilson, and mind, don't wait for me to-night."

A look of deep gloom and disappointment was visible on the man's face, as he went his way, his heart too full to make an intelligible reply ; but, once out of his master's hearing, the pent-up words broke forth.

" Next mail, poor lad ; she'll not write, the heartless hussy ! That I should say such words of her ! But she'll be gaddin' about London, I'll be bound ; carin' for any one else but her own flesh and blood. Such women don't deserve to be mothers. Her only child, too. And Mr. Gerard to be in the power of one as treats him so !"

Alone with himself, Gerard dressed leisurely, and bestowed more than ordinary attention upon his usually fastidious toilette. His thick, short-cropped brown hair, shot with the faintest tinge of chestnut, was brushed carefully aside from off his low broad forehead, and for the last time he peered in the glass, which reflected a face few women would have considered aught but handsome, and many an one would not have cared to scorn. Young it certainly was, and as yet the depths of his dark blue eyes wore two expressions good to look upon — truth and honesty. It was time to go, and he went downstairs, and entered the gharry which was in waiting for him, directing the man where to drive to with a smile on his frank, boyish features. The distance was soon accomplished, and a black servant flung open the drawing-room door, and announced " Clarencourt Sahib," as he ushered him into a large, lofty apartment, richly furnished, but, save for a few soft, bright coloured rugs, *objets d'art* of Eastern manufacture, and the heavy waving folds of the punkah, like, in all other respects, an ordinary reception-room at home. Englishmen, wherever they go, seldom fail to carry their habits and their customs with them; and an Anglo-Indian hugs and treasures up his recollections of life in the old country, and endeavours, in most cases, to make his foreign one resemble it as much as is in accordance with the change of climate.

As Gerard stood and surveyed his surroundings, naturally enough expecting to find her who had been in his thoughts so much of late, he was astonished to see no one, and was about to look for his conductor, to inquire where his mistress was, when his ears were gladdened by the rustle of a dress and the sound of a voice he knew.

"How do you do, Mr. Clarencourt? I was about to despair of your coming," and advancing towards him from behind some ferns where she had remained hidden, Ada Devereaux extended a fair white hand, the shapely fingers of which sparkled with diamonds, and Clarencourt, as he pressed it in his, and looked upon her tall, voluptuous, but stately figure, from which every trace of girlhood and awkwardness had vanished and lost itself in the rounded outline and more splendid magnificence of the woman, felt that he had *not* deceived himself. She was a

blonde, with strikingly classical features, blue
eyes of a turquoise hue, and bright, golden
hair coiled about her head in a way which
concealed its masses, but enhanced the
piquant expression of her face. In the whole
course of his short life Gerard, as he gazed
at her, thought that never had he seen a
being so radiantly beautiful. She perceived
the look and smiled in triumph as she read
him through, and saw her victory written in
his eyes.

"You could not think so ill of me, Mrs.
Devereaux," he stammered in answer to her
remark.

"Not ill of *you*, no! but I feared that you
might have some other engagement. But do
you know, Mr. Clarencourt, I think it so
stupid of people to disappoint one just at the
last moment. Colonel and Mrs. Montagu
Thomson were to have been here to-night
to meet you, and this afternoon, quite late, I
received a note requesting me to excuse them,
on some slight pretext, I forget now what it
was, but you know I had no time to ask

any one else. I thought of your friend Mr. Carelesse, but feared that he might be engaged too, so there is no one here. Shall you mind so dreadfully dull an ordeal as a *tête-à-tête* dinner with me ? " As she asked him, Ada Devereaux raised her head, and in her eyes, as they met his, there shone the light and expression which she so well knew how to assume. Before the witchery of that glance older and more experienced men than Gerard Clarencourt had been forced to lower their colours and submit to an ignominious surrender. She was fully aware of the potency of its subtle charms, and she saw that in this case also she had not overrated its effect. A tinge of colour suffused Gerard's cheeks, and his eyes sparkled, but in all other respects he was calm outwardly.

" Mrs. Devereaux, you know that to be here gives me the greatest pleasure ; as for the society of others, if *mine* won't bore *you* I would far rather be without them." He spoke honestly, as he felt, and she did know it, but she uttered a low rippling laugh.

"Mr. Clarencourt, although I believe you are not an Irishman, that finished compliment cannot be meant, but am I to learn to treat you as I do Mr. Carelesse? I have never known when he does mean what he says, so I studiously doubt it all."

"Then, need I entreat you not to judge me so harshly," answered Gerard, as he offered his arm and felt a nervous thrill of pleasure as her hand rested within it, and he led her to a seat at the daintily laid table, resplendent with silver, and decorated in a style of tasteful elegance with rare and beautiful flowers. The dinner passed off with the usual chit-chat, and the servants were watchful and attentive as only blacks can be; the secret of it is no doubt that they know their social position and are not forced out of the sphere in which nature intended them to move. They don't ape their betters and have learnt the lesson of obedience. Once Gerard remarked during the meal:

"You like flowers, Mrs. Devereaux."

"I am intensely fond of them. I spend

half my spare time in attempting to grow them to perfection. You shall see my garden, and I think you will agree with me that it is lovely." Later in the evening, as Gerard hung over her at the piano and turned the pages of her music, she looked up and said :

"Are you fond of singing, Mr. Clarencourt?" for hitherto she had played nothing but instrumental music, and Gerard had listened in admiration as she had executed piece after piece, with a soft brilliancy of touch added to a correctness of rendering and a pathos which held him spell-bound to her side, and he had not thought of asking her whether she sang.

" I love it," he murmured simply. Then, without pausing save to strike a few bold chords, she burst into a low, sweet, passionate refrain, and her clear soprano voice rose and fell in rich, mellow cadence, which echoed through the room and passed out into the night, rousing the half-slumbering servants, as they lolled full length on their mats, under the shadow of the verandah, and making them raise their listless bodies and listen, drinking in each sound as though it were the voice of a houri, come to them from the visionary paradise of their dreams. Several songs she sang for him, and he had only stammered out his thanks in simple phrases, for his very soul was enraptured by the music, and he longed to hear more of that gentle melody which seemed to him to possess in it something of the supernatural.

"You like to hear me sing," she said as she rose from the instrument.

"I have never heard a voice I liked so much," he answered gently. "I suppose you will think me guilty of flattery when I say so, Mrs. Devereaux, but I can assure you I mean every word I say."

"Then I will believe you," she said softly; and as he stood before her, and drank in the subtle perfume of her golden tresses, and gazed into those eyes which seemed to him so good and true and yet withal so lovely to look upon, Gerard Clarencourt felt that whether for good or evil, whether for weal or woe, this woman could do with him as she liked.

CHAPTER III.

HIS VOW.

As he had bid her good-bye, and passed out into the moonlit garden, he had heard her last words as in a dream.

" Come in and see me whenever you care to, Mr. Clarencourt ; we must not be strangers, you know." But so preoccupied was he that without knowing it he had almost brushed with his coat sleeve the arm of a man who was standing behind the trunk of a palm, and who was regarding him with a face convulsed by passion and jealousy. He looked as if he could have shot him dead, with as little compunction as he would have poured the contents of his double-barrelled breechloader into the bodies of a brace of luckless snipe, to pick them up with a laugh and reload again to continue the slaughter.

That man was Geoffrey Carelesse.

"So that was your little game," he muttered, as he watched Gerard's retreating
figure until it was hidden from him by a
clump of shrubs. "That was why you
wanted to write letters, and refused to dine
with me. But to add insult to injury you
must try to throw me off the scent by asking
me to meet you. That was your reason for
sending me your infernal letter of apology,
couched in friendly terms, and all so d——d
suave. By heaven, I hate you!" Fortunate it
was that Gerard did not see or hear him, for
Carelesse was half mad with temper, and most
assuredly had they met then there would
have been blood shed. But he was oblivious
of it all. Exalted above the trivialities of his
every day existence, into a heaven created
by his own bright unfettered imagination, he
seemed to tread lightly as on air, while
whirling through his brain in wild confusion
were her words and actions, as he strove to
separate and conjure them before him one by
one, and echoing through the still night air,

he seemed to hear again that glorious voice, and before him rose the form of the woman he had left. He was happy, happier than he had ever felt before. And yet, he could scarce have told himself why. He had not paused to reason or to think. He did not want to do so. He only knew he felt strangelo light-hearted, and it was enough. Had he been told that his joy had been brought about by a woman whom he scarcely knew, and had not known, or even met, one short week ago, he would have laughed with scorn. He was rich, well-clad, well-fed, well-cared for. In the middle of the road, only a few yards distant from him, moved a solitary figure. It was that of a man like himself, but oh, how different! In place of the wealth he was dependent upon the charity of others, and he hungered now. His body was covered by the thinnest covering of muslin rags, and he dragged his weary, pain-racked limbs along the dusty road, in misery. Light streamed from behind a cloud, and shone upon his thin, worn, emaciated countenance.

4—2

Great shapeless blotches of a dazzling whiteness marked his skin. This man was a leper
shunned by his fellow-men, who fled from him
as from a thing accursed. Because of the
terrible nature of his loathsome disease, an
outcast. Doomed to a living death before
the tomb had closed upon him. For ever
isolated from the world, and,—dare we say it?
dare we even think it?—for a time at least, perhaps condemned and left alone by God. How
ghastly, how awful! What a life in death!
And yet the same moon shone upon them
both. Dives and Lazarus were not a greater
contrast. *Mes frères*, think on it, and thank
God it was not your fate. Why should you
not have been a leper, *white* as that man?
But to return to Carelesse. After Gerard had
disappeared he only waited in his hiding-
place until he had been able to collect his
thoughts and calm himself. Then with
steady and deliberate tread he walked up to
the door of the bungalow, and pulled the bell.

"Better see her now, and hear from her
own lips her perfidy," he muttered.

" The white lady no see you, sar," replied the Hindu, in answer to his request to see Mrs. Devereaux. He knew that the hour was late, and that his behaviour was anything but that of an officer and a gentleman, yet he strode past the servant and entered the drawing-room. Mrs. Devereaux was reclining negligently on a sofa, with the mellow and subdued rays of a shaded lamp, which stood upon a low ebony table at her side, throwing its pale radiance upon her rounded cheek. One hand supported her head, the other held a novel, the contents of which seemed to please her much, for as Carelesse entered the room, unnoticed by her, so intent was she upon her book, a mellow peal of laughter broke from her lips.

" Well, it is irresistibly funny," she said aloud to herself. The mirth and the sound of her voice made Carelesse start as if bitten by a serpent, but by a powerful effort he controlled his feelings and crossed the room towards her. The noise of his footsteps were heard by the occupant of the lounge. At first she did not see him, her sight was dazzled

by the sudden transition from the light by
which she had read to the partial gloom
which enveloped the rest of the apartment.
Then she saw his face, and started to her feet
with surprise.

" You here, Mr. Carelesse."

" Yes, it is I."

" And by what earthly right, may I ask, do
you venture *here*, and unannounced intrude
upon my privacy ? "

" Simply because I wished to see and speak
with you.   I have no other excuse to offer."

" Then the reason is not ample enough.
Am I to be disturbed at your will and for
your pleasure?   You tamper with my patience
sorely if you think so."

" Ada, listen to me for five minutes."

" Certainly, Mr. Carelesse ; but pray end this
absurd scene."   She had sunk back into her
former seat upon the sofa, and the expression
of her face was one of splendid indifference,
and well-assumed contempt.   Her white teeth
were clenched upon her full, red, pouting lips,
as if to enable her to stifle the indignation

which caused her full and beautifully moulded
bosom to rise and fall under its covering of
lace. Motionless she sat, her eyes flashing
with a dangerous steel-blue light, and her foot
beating in quick spasmodic jerks against the
polished floor. Carelesse, as he looked, thought
that never had she seemed so lovely. How he
longed to take her in his arms and press the
mouth he loved to look upon to his, in one
long passionate kiss, to know that she was
true, and his! for he cared for her better than
his life. Then he burst forth :

"Why did you ask that boy Clarencourt
to dine with you?" If Carelesse, as he put the
question, thought for one moment that he was
likely to receive an answer he was very much
mistaken.

"Mr. Carelesse, if you have any civil remark
to make, pray let me hear it. Have you left
all trace of the gentleman behind you at your
mess table?"

"By heaven, you'll drive me mad! For
what good purpose did you invite him here,
to dine with him alone? I suppose you are

delighted with his graceful figure and charmingly unsophisticated manner. Something new, eh, and fancy yourself in love?"

"Well, suppose I were?"

"Why, I would shoot him with as little compunction as I would a cur." Each moment, as Carelesse grew more and more infuriated, and less able after every sentence to control himself, Mrs. Devereaux became calmer; she saw her advantage and was too clever not to seize it. It is often so with a woman.

"How very heroic!" she murmured, as though she were answering some trivial remark. "Quite brave of you," she continued. "The only drawback to the pleasure you meditate giving yourself would be the chance that he *might* shoot you, unless you did it from behind a tree."

White with fury Carelesse thought it was time to play his last card, but as he did it blind with wrath he robbed himself of any chance he had, or might ever have possessed of ruling Ada Devereaux's will.

"See here ; do you know who I am?"

" Geoffrey Carelesse, I suppose, unless you happen to be *alias* some one else."

"Shall I tell you who you are, or rather were before you married Colonel Devereaux?"

It was his turn now, and he watched every vestige of colour desert her face, and saw her draw her breath in quick short gasps, while her fingers clutched the lace handkerchief she held, and nervously tore and crumpled it. She could scarcely articulate, so well had the arrow been directed, and so thoroughly had its barbed point pierced the only vulnerable joint in her armour, and forcing its way, spite of her will, buried itself deep down in her very heart's core. It was a cruel shot, for which she had been prepared in no way. She had been surprised and attacked from a quarter whence she least expected an assault. Against such odds, what wonder that even she—clever woman though she undoubtedly was—succumbed for the instant?

" You ; what do *you* know about me ? " she asked, with a sickly attempt at a smile, and a fruitless effort to appear calm.

" All, everything."

The brief reply gave her courage. How should he know? Here was no accusation. Perhaps he had thought by random words, based upon no foundation, to get her in his power. He should see how miserably he had failed.

"Everything means nothing, Mr. Carelesse. Of my past life I am not ashamed, and there is no incident in it which I would not lay bare before the world. I do not fear its censure, and I am not likely to shrink before yours. But you have made a base insinuation, and before you quit this house to-night you shall explain yourself."

She had recovered her nerve, and as she stared him full in the face she hissed forth each word with withering scorn. Carelesse, as he stood before her, and saw the fury of the tempest he had raised, already began to doubt his power to soothe or subdue it. The words had scarce left his lips before he began to regret ever having spoken. He loved her, and what if in his jealous anger he had roused

the storm which should recoil like the boome-
rang, back upon himself, and wreck his life.
What if she would *not* forgive him. The
thought brought great beads of perspiration
to his forehead.

"Ada Devereaux," he answered, and the
tones of his voice were gentle; "there are
things which were better left unsaid. Don't
probe too deep. I am passionate, I know,
but let us forget what *has* passed, and say
no more on the subject." He could not
have made a more fatal error. To attempt
to pacify, having once begun the fight,
before he had taught a lesson, was absurd;
he was already crying *peccavi*. He had
wilfully stirred up a wasp's nest, and then
was afraid to meet the sting. He had
landed troops in an enemy's country, and
the first onslaught cooled his ardour and
made him long to withdraw his forces by
the best and safest roads. She saw her
advantage, and more than ever was impressed with the idea that she had been
alarmed without a cause. He had com-

menced the retrograde movement. He was a coward, and she would force an explanation from him. She had quite regained her composure now, and was herself again.

"Yes, I dare say *you* would like to insult me, and then offer no explanation. It is worthy of you. Were I a man, I would *force* one from you; as a woman, I *ask* you as a gentleman to explain your words and the insinuation they contained. If you refuse I shall, painful though it may be to me, consider that I have opened my doors to, and unwittingly associated with a man, not only a disgrace to his sex, but to the army he has entered. Had you spoken the words you have in this room during Colonel Devereaux's lifetime he would have had you horsewhipped from the door. Is my language plain enough, Mr. Carelesse? There is my accusation; *now*, have the goodness to tell me yours."

Carelesse was no coward. The biting sarcasm cut him to the quick. It was with difficulty he controlled his rage.

" You wish to hear what I know? "

" I insist upon it."

" Do you remember Brunsmure Terrace, South Kensington, and some people of the name of Dailey? "

" Perfectly."

" Then, I am Geoffrey Dailey."

" How can you prove such an assertion? " she asked in a tremulous voice and with a face from which every vestige of colour had again fled.

" Very simply. I have merely assumed the name of Carclesse at the request of my uncle, with whom I went to live soon after you left us. You are Ada Blanchard. Naturally enough you did not recognize me out here and under another name; besides, it is years since you saw me, and I was a mere boy at the time when you——"

" I—I do not doubt you. And I do not de—deny your assertion. I am Ada Blanchard. But I see no further use in prolonging this discussion; if you wish to injure me——"

" *I injure you!* why, Ada ; can you deem me guilty of such cowardice ? "

" If you are not, what was your reason for mentioning this painful subject ? You may have heard too, since you know so much about me, that I was more sinned against than sinning. Mr. Eagles——"

" For heaven's sake, say no more. I know what a brute he was to you, and that he deserted you like the black-hearted villain he was. But, Ada, will you try to forget all that my foolish words conveyed? It was jealousy which caused me to speak so hotly." She heard his voice and what he said distinctly, but she made no answer It might be better, perhaps, for her to be on the safe side with this man. It would be a terrible *exposé* if the whole facts of the case were known publicly, as he had it in his power to tell them. Society in Calcutta would not be disposed to view with a lenient eye the peccadilloes of her youth. She had too many enemies, as a pretty woman, amongst those of her own sex, who envied her for her good looks, and who would gladly seize and gloat over any piece of scandal which would enable them to pick her to pieces. Besides, although she did not care for the man the least bit in the world, it would be easy to make him think so. She well knew that he loved her, and while that was the case he would scarcely malign her to others. So long as she could keep up the farce she was safe from him. *Finesse* was clearly her game, she argued within herself during the dead silence which had ensued between them. Carelesse was the first to break it.

"I am waiting for an answer; will you give it me? Can you pardon me for my harsh, unkind words? You may judge how much I love you; only the other day, by the merest chance, I discovered who you were. You had left your davenport open, and on it was lying a birthday book. I examined it from pure curiosity, and I can swear to you, with no wish to pry into any secrets of yours; on the fly-leaf I saw the

name of Ada Blanchard in a handwriting I
recognized only too well, for the lines were
penned by my dead sister, and the book
was a gift from her to you. I turned to
the date of my own birthday, and there
I read my name, written in a crabbed,
boyish hand, but nevertheless my own signature, without doubt. The chain of evidence
was complete. Passion only caused me to
speak to you as I have done, for I swore
to keep my discovery a secret. Ada, I
loved you before I saw that book. I love
you now. God only knows how dearly.
One thing I swear, and rest assured I shall
keep this oath, whether you forgive me or
not ; whether you see fit to love me or no.
Remember my vow. No man shall rob me
of you and live." There came a day when
both recalled those words and their fatal
meaning but too vividly. "Can you forgive me?" he asked in a low voice, broken
by emotion.

"On one condition I will."

"And it is?"

"That you promise never to disclose my former name while you live. If you love me as you say, you could not wish to do me an injury."

"I promise you on my honour," he answered simply; yet she knew and felt that the secret of her former life was as safe as though it was hidden in the tomb.

"I know I was a fool to mistrust you, Ada, yet it was love for you alone which prompted me to speak of Clarencourt. I long for the time to come, and it cannot surely be so very far distant, for my uncle is an old man now, when I shall possess a purse ample enough for me to know that your every wish and trifling whim can be satisfied. Then I shall lay it and my love together at your feet. Oh, that the day would come! Might I hope, my darling?" Mrs. Devereaux's head was slightly averted, and there was a dead pause of some seconds ere she turned to reply. In her inmost heart she hated this man; yes, positively hated him. Why had her evil genius brought her into contact with *him*, who, above all others, with the exception of one or two of his own kith and kin, she would have shunned, and fled from as from a pestilence? Did *he* not know—was he not possessed of the knowledge of that one error of her life, that had transformed her—confiding and trusting enough before, willing to have staked her existence and all but her honour rather than doubt his plighted word —into a perfect woman of the world, unimpressionable, cold, calculating, with a heart hard as adamant, and glorying in its possession, because it enabled her to wreak her vengeance upon any of the sex whom she might meet? They had robbed her of her first young love, had flung it back upon her as a thing worthless, to be despised, to be rejected. She had never forgotten or forgiven the brutal insult. Henceforth (she had told herself), men should be her tools, and she had kept faith with herself, and had uttered a ringing laugh as she left them bowed down and stricken at her feet, because of the beauty they coveted passing them by unscathed. In her case, the contaminating influence of earth's touch was too plainly evident. The clay, as God had sent it here, had been, as it ever is, *pure*, but plastic, soft and yielding. Those by whom it had been surrounded and brought into closest contact had fallen short in their duties, had handled it roughly, had failed to engraft into it the good they should, but had rather impregnated it with evil, harshness, in place of kindness, and a wanton lack of governing principle where the firm pressure of the curb should have been used. The fair surface of that life had been dented, bruised and cruelly battered, and it had grown up the thing it was.

Well did Mrs. Devereaux know that the man at her side loved her with an adoration beside which all other circumstances of his being were as naught. Yet the knowledge did not make her shrink from her task. It might endanger her own safety to release him from his bondage, to tell him openly and straightforwardly that she never could be anything to him. If she trusted in his honour alone, and sent him away with the truth ringing in his ears, he might change his *rôle* of lover for that of her bitterest foe. No, she must deceive him. Her line of conduct once marked out and decided upon, nothing would induce her to alter her tactics. So she listened to his whisperings, answering him with honeyed sayings, and suffered his kiss, while from her very soul she loathed him. He left her that night, and sought his solitary quarters more securely chained and manacled, if possible, than ever, her slave for life, while she retired to her chamber and unrobed, drawing the clinging folds of the mosquito curtains about her to shield her dainty limbs from poisonous stings, without one prayer that her sins might be forgiven her.

CHAPTER IV.

ACROSS the warm, limpid waters of the Bay of Bengal, on and on, thousands of miles, away from the muddy current of the Hooghly, we must wander, in thought, until before us tower the tall red cliffs of southern Devon. Ride on the summit of one of those rollers which chafe over a hidden reef, brown and jagged, keen and merciless as monster sharks' teeth to the tempest-tossed mariner, whose drowning agony they have silently witnessed, and of whose death-shriek, grim and awful, in its intensity of anguish, their hard, tempest-covered masses have been the cause. Pass on in safety and land on the golden stretch of sand, where the mighty volume of foam-flecked heaving water has hurled you, sound of

limb and unharmed. The whining cries of
a tiny Blenheim spaniel disturb the still,
solemn silence broken before by the swish
of the waves alone. Evidently the dog had
strayed to play upon a large, detached frag-
ment of rock which, perhaps in ages past,
had formed a portion of the reef, but having
been torn off by the fury of the sea, and
tossed upon the land, had become firmly
embedded. The tide had rushed swiftly in,
and one wave, mightier than its fellows,
had spent its fury on the base of the rock,
a portion of it, eddying round, had filled a
trench which nature had hollowed about it,
and thus the dog's retreat was cut off.
Afraid to make its escape when the danger
first menaced it, it had shrunk from dipping
its dainty paws into the chill, salt water
until to have attempted it would have meant
a determined bound and a swim of several
feet, courage for which the training it had
been subjected to had not instilled. So it
moaned and howled in piteous lamentation,
its round prominent eyes almost starting

from its head in terror. Some distance off a girl, with block and brush, was busy sketching, and by her side lay strewn upon the shingle odds and ends, brushes and paints, a novel, and a mantle soft and warm, placed there, no doubt, to shield the puny limbs of the dog from harm, for amongst its folds peeped forth a silver collar, bearing this simple inscription, " Lilian Fabyn." The sun was sinking westward, and a flood of gorgeous rays streamed on the sparkling, limitless expanse which stretched away far as the eye could reach, a dim haze blending both sky and sea at length in one broad belt of misty colouring. Here and there the brilliant shimmering light fell slant-wise on the brown-sailed fishing trawler gone to its nightly toil, and in further distance still, it lingered with its golden beams on square-rigged merchantmen outward bound to far-off climes. The cotton sails of an American trader looked white and glistening, clearly limned against the horizon, as struggling against a brisk head wind she beat her way

with many a tack up channel. The scene
was one of striking beauty, and Lilian Fabyn's
face, for she it was, caught something of
the painter's glow of enthusiasm as she
strove to transfer to her canvas, with broad
bold touch, the ever-changing shadows and
bright effects before her. Something of in-
spiration, as she bent over her canvas, and
her eyes bore that far-away expression,
though sparkling with interest and enthusiasm, that never comes save when one's
thoughts and feelings are concentrated in
an art they love to follow, in a duty where
heart and soul are one, and lend their combined energies to aid each other in a grand
effort to complete the task begun. It was
easy to see that she was absorbed, nay,
rather *lost*, in her work; added to this the
wind was blowing from a direction which
carried the sharp, snappish barks and howls
of the dog away from her, and these two
causes were sufficient to account for his
melancholy position as he wandered round
the confined limits of his self-made prison.

The spray had already begun to wet his glossy coat, and piteous tears filled his round, distended eyes, now protruding fearfully from fright and nervous terror, when his young mistress stretched out her left hand, more from habit, probably, than any other reason, and without relinquishing her brush, to caress her pet. It rested on the folds of the cloak alone ; this made her lift her eyes from her drawing to look for him. No, he was not there. Half upsetting her easel, in her anxiety and alarm at his supposed loss, she rose to her feet, and with a hurried glance scanned the stretch of beach in front of her. He was nowhere to be seen. Turning hastily, with her hand raised to shade her sight from the glinting sunbeams, she saw him.

"Poor Rex, you stupid dog, how *did* you get there?" burst from her lips, as she took in the whole situation at a glance.

In another instant she ran fast as her lithe, graceful limbs could carry her, to the rescue, regardless of the risk to herself as she bounded, light as a chamois, over green weed-covered boulders, treading on a luckless crab or star-fish, and clearing at a bound deep crannies and miniature pools, where lurked the finest prawns to be found on the coast, and red, green and purple sea anemones innumerable. She never stopped until she stood as close as the incoming tide would allow her to the wretched, shivering little animal.

"Never mind, Rexy, you poor, silly little doggie, you shan't even wet your paws," she continued, and without hesitation proceeded to untie and throw aside her dainty shoes and silken stockings.

What was it to her to plunge her pretty pink feet and shapely limbs into the brine? She had been born and bred by the sea, and only a few short years back would have liked nothing better than to be allowed to roam at will, undisturbed and without restriction, permitted to spend half her day amongst the hidden mysteries of that tempest-torn, sea-swept reef. What was it now? She might have, by dint of persuasion and threats, induced the dog to commit himself to the water he so much dreaded, but then it would have given him pain, and she would a thousand times rather have borne it herself than cause any dumb animal in existence a moment's misery. So with cautious steps she picked her way, for the sharp, broken edges of the shingle made her clench her teeth and give vent to many an " Oh ! " of torture, as splintered particles and rough brown rock punctured her tender skin. She had sunk above her knees, and the waves had splashed her dress and saturated the edges of it, but it gave her not an instant's thought. She caught the dog in her arms and strained him to her as if he were the best friend she had on earth. Perhaps he was ; for while he had breath in his body he would, true to his canine instincts, have followed her to the utmost limits of the earth, whether she were rich or poor, whether good or bad befell her, so long as she suffered him he would leave her for no other. A last crust he would have shared a morsel of, and when death overtook him, drawn his last gasp, and gazed into her face, and tried to show his delight at the touch of the hand he loved by a last wag of his silky tail. And tell me, you who know life, you who have seen *most* of its ups and downs, where will you find such fidelity? where will you find such an im- plicit trust? where will you find such a true love in a human being? Then, assuredly, it is but seldom. It was a pleas- ing sight and fair to look upon, that glad young face, so hopeful, so blooming, so radiant with health and strength—typical of life as it sets out on its journey — with the tiny, long, soft-haired Blenheim fawn- ing about her, licking her hands, jumping upon her lap, as she sought to arrange her dress, then wildly running around her, as if mad with delight, and unable to testify with its gambols and short metallic barks of pleasure, all it felt and would say if it could have spoken. Had some of her London friends seen Lilian Fabyn just then, they might have gained an insight into her character, and have understood in a measure why she cared for her country home, and told them of her wish to return to it; why she sickened and grew tired of the endless round of gaiety of her first London season; why she preferred a canter on her mare by the lone sea shore, rather than a crowded ball-room or a fashionable crush. Her eyes had not been blinded as yet; she read it and estimated it at its worth. It was all too painfully hollow, and its dazzling brilliancy had altogether failed, in those few weeks of her stay in town, to cast its glamour about her. She had sighed, ere half of it had passed, for the breezy woods, and the endless soothing sound of the waves, and had teased her father, kind cheery-hearted Sir George, into returning, spite of himself and the oft-repeated assertion which had escaped Lady Fabyn's lips, that Lilian would never be married and that she was not to be so easily coerced into going back to Sidcombe, when everybody was enjoying themselves!

The idea was ridiculous, and not to be thought of ; so said Lady Fabyn. If Lilian chose to ruin her prospects she must do so, but she would be no party to it. She had moped down at that wretched place for months, and it would positively kill her if she were obliged to endure it again so soon. To the first remark, about Lilian's marriage, Sir George had replied in a thoroughly characteristic speech :

"What matter, wife ? Time enough for the girl yet. Think I want some muff, because he has a handle to his name and plenty of rupees, but who can't ride a yard, and doesn't know a good bit of horseflesh when he sees it, to come spooning my daughter? I don't want some white-faced boy, with a bandolined thing he calls a moustache, to make love to Lilian because he is tired of sowing his wild oats, and his mother tells him that *really* it is time he thought seriously of matrimony, and looked out for a nice young woman of good family with some money, and then puts him on to my girl;

so there's an end of it. Now Lilian would stay up here like a shot because you want to, but *I* don't; I'm sick of it, and for once I'm going to be a bit selfish and leave you to the tender mercies of Lady Bracebridge. I know she is dying to see you—always is, and you two hit it off together splendidly. So drop a line or, better still, keep on the house, if you won't find it dull, and Lilian and I will just get clear of all this dust and bother."

This little discussion had taken place a day or two after Lilian had written the letter to Gerard Clarencourt which had found him at the Great Eastern Hotel, Calcutta. Sir George had only been too delighted to discover some pretext for a removal back to Devonshire, and a chance word or two dropped by Lilian had laid the foundation for the excuse which they had acted upon. If some of Lilian Fabyn's admirers had chanced to have seen the little incident of Rex's deliverance from begining to end, it strikes me that they would have gone home, certainly, not less in love with her. For what men admire most in a woman, and I venture to think that I am committing no blunder when I say so, is gentleness, tenderness, a capacity for love, in one word womanliness, or what one has been taught to construe as such.

It might be as well to look more closely at Lilian Fabyn as she walked back along the beach, her brown and white coloured pet hugged closely in her arms, as if she feared to lose him again. She certainly was pretty; none could deny that; even those who envied her good looks were forced to admit as much, and any unprejudiced person, who could see straight, would probably have said more in her favour. Tall in figure, though well-shaped, and not the least gawky. Her hair was brown, and, where the sun glinted on it, shot with golden. A neat, quiet straw hat, round which was a white ribbon, did not conceal the fact that she had small, straight-cut features. The mouth perhaps just a trifle large, but that blemish

more than atoned for by even rows of teeth
of pearly hue, and firmly, though with a
kindly look, her full, pink lips closed over
them. Her eyes were brown as a ripe hazel-
nut, and scarcely ever wore the same expression long together. They danced with
laughter and merriment one moment, and
the next were dreamy and listless or melting,
just as the thought seized her. A face which
seen once was not forgotten easily. As she
resumed her seat again before her easel
and drew her colours near, her full, round,
girlish figure showed to advantage, clad as
she was in a simple tight-fitting blue dress of
thin texture and clinging material. The dog
had coiled himself up snugly on the cloak,
and she had strapped round his neck the
silver collar graven with her name, and
resumed her brush, evidently with the intention of continuing her painting. For
some few minutes she busied herself by
scanning the landscape before her, but it
seemed only too apparent that the beauty
of the day had vanished with the sun as it

sank behind the heights, which rose pre
cipitously in some parts directly from the
level of the beach, darkest Indian red in
tint, now that the shades of evening approached, yet still left their summits bathed
in brightest orange rays, as if loth to rob
them of their borrowed beauty.

"Time you and I were thinking of going
homewards, Rex," she said, as she patted his
glossy coat. "That little escapade of yours
has stolen the best part of the afternoon from
me, and now I shall have to make a point
of coming down here again before I can
finish this sketch. No matter, I forgive you,
you old dear. Supposing some monster wave
had come, and carried you away with it,
what should I have done? I don't believe
anything could console me for your loss."

Talking thus to her dog she packed up all
her artistic paraphernalia into as small a
space as possible, and then, with her companion under her arm, crossed the rough
pebbles, and began to ascend a narrow,
winding path, which was cut in the cliff,

and seemed to be the only means of reaching the top, any more circuitous route which might have existed along the shore apparently being cut off by the rapid influx of the tide. Patches of yellow gorse grew thick on either hand, blue and other gay-coloured butterflies fluttered from bush to bush, and high in the azure vault of heaven soared the larks, filling the air with their sweet ringing songs. The scene was one of infinite peace. The face of nature seemed to repose in that sublime and solemn stillness which is more noticeable towards the close of the day, when all work is laid aside, when the industrious mechanics in the country village, the shrewd man of business in the thronging, densely-populated city, worn and fatigued with his struggle to obtain gold, and the bronzed and healthy-looking farm labourer, tired with his heavy toil, lay aside their several implements of labour, to seek their firesides and the smiles of those they love, as the shadows of evening fall, and the brief respite comes to strengthen and arm them with fresh might for the morrow's trials. And to stand on the crest of the high precipitous cliffs of Sidcombe, as Lilian did, from sheer love of the beauties so lavishly scattered around her, could bring no other feeling to the heart than rest. Down, far down, hundreds of feet below her, the sea beat upon the sand, with ceaseless monotony, as if never tired of chafing against its smooth surface. Never tired of lashing it, in its resistless strength, yet powerless to outstep by one foot its appointed limits. She could scarcely discern the foam-capped breakers which swept over the treacherous rocks, so far was she above them, and a score of cable-lengths from the shore the water looked calm as an inland lake ; seagulls, as they fought and croaked their harsh discordant cries over the cast-up morsels of offal, and pounced upon the young, unwary fish, were only the smallest specks of white. Inland, the view that met her gaze was not one whit less beautiful, or less worthy of notice. Green, rolling uplands, cool depths

of shade, where the oak and ash grew side
by side with the straight-stemmed fir,
covering many an acre of hill and dale.
And faint wreaths of bluish smoke curled
upwards, and showed where the thatched
roof of a homestead lurked. The silver
windings of a river could be traced as it
unfolded its snaky coils, partly hidden in
places by a dip in the land, or by thick over-
hanging larches, and the distant horizon was
marked by a range of cone-shaped tors, high,
and of a purple tinge in the ambient light.
The girl drew in a deep breath of the strong
exhilarating air, which savoured of the peaty
heights of Exmoor and the scent of wood
fires, and then hastened on along a narrow
sheep track, through thin, wiry herbage and
patches of wild thyme, until a slope of the
hill brought her by a gradual descent to the
banks of the stream. The spaniel had
struggled to the ground, and was trotting
along behind her, pausing at times to raise its
head and utter a shrill chorus of barks as a
rabbit, scared by the sound of approaching

footsteps, scudded off to seek its burrow. A rustic footbridge enabled her to cross to the other side, and then before her stretched a long vista of running water, bounding and splashing, descending in miniature cascades, and falling into deep pools, which time had hollowed in its rocky bed, where the red-spotted trout hid from their enemy the otter, or rose lazily to the surface in sport to suck in and gorge themselves with flies which happened to excite their fickle fancy. She paused for an instant to open a white-painted iron gate, which led her on to a stretch of turf, dotted with giant yews, old as the days when the archers used the pliant wood to make their bows. Ten minutes uphill walking and she had entered a quaint old-fashioned, terraced garden, gay with the cultured blooms of standard roses. An old, round-backed, aged man was bending over one of these, intent upon destroying the insects collected on the branches; he was either pre-occupied with his work, or, more likely still, deaf; as he failed to hear the sounds made by Lilian as she drew near.

"Well, Budd," she said, addressing the gardener; "have you discovered another tree injured by that nasty blight?"

"Yes, miss. The *insecks* is all over it; there's no keeping of 'em off. I'm thinking that they'll not be so fine as they was last year, Miss Lilian, and it's put me about, 'cause Sir George is set on getting the first prize, and he don't take beatin' kindly."

"Oh, never fear, Budd, you will be sure to win it. It is quite an institution; they would not think of giving it to any one else." The man turned his face, which reminded one in hue and shape of a crushed, red-cheeked cider apple, so full of knots and wrinkles was it, yet he looked the picture of health.

"We don't want no favour, Miss Lilian, from any one; we wants to stand on our merits. Those are the very words I mind your grandpa made use of when he took the short-horn prizes for seven years."

"Were they?" She had heard him make

the same remark scores of times before. "Well, Budd, you'll get the prize, I am sure."

"The Clarencourt man, the new chap as they have, is doin' his best, so I've heerd." Lilian Fabyn made some suitable reply, but turned quickly, and hurried up a flight of stone steps leading to a broad sweep of gravel which curved round in front of the house. The bare mention of the name, so unexpectedly alluded to by the garrulous old servant, brought a blush to her cheek she did not care for him to see, and yet somehow could not control. Had the question been asked her, and answered frankly, she would have been forced to admit that she thought of Gerard Clarencourt more than the demands of simple friendship required.

"Why was it so?" she would ask herself. He had never shown any decided preference for her more than the mere dictates of an old acquaintanceship as near neighbours demanded. And yet the germ had been planted in her heart and had grown slowly, but none the less surely. When Gerard had bid her good-bye a day or two before he started on his travels, it was then, as she saw him saunter off with a careless laugh and a wave of his hat, that she knew and felt how much she should miss his face. And as week after week had passed, each to her seeming longer than the one preceding it, she had grown weary and dejected in spirit. She never argued herself into believing that he loved her; his actions told her too plainly that such was not the case. In vain had she summoned pride to aid her in dismissing his image from her memory; the attempt had ended in a miserable failure, and she had fallen back, like many another, on the oft-tried mainstay, hope. Hope that in the long years to come he would love her.

The grand old pile of masonry which was known to the country side as The Towers, and which had owned the sway of many succeeding generations of Fabyns long before a title had been granted to one of them for success in arms, was perhaps, from an architectural point of view, one of the queerest medleys to be

met with in the southern counties. The
original portion of the building had consisted
of one strongly-built tower having walls many
feet thick, and loop-holed for purposes of
defence. There existed still a divided opinion
as to its date, but that it was very ancient
there could be no doubt. As time wore on,
and each fresh owner had grown in wealth, to
this solitary structure had been added, for the
sake of convenience here, or appearance there,
just as the fit had seized them, new wings,
turrets and buttresses, protruding in one place,
receding at another, full of sharp angles,
rounded corners and sheltered nooks. The
oldest part of the edifice was covered to its
battlements with ivy, the roots of which had
grown to an enormous thickness; the more
modern, which was especially occupied by the
present family, overtwined by masses of thick,
close-growing creepers, the bright-coloured,
red-leaved American and others, japonicas,
passion flowers and clematis. On the opposite side to that on which Lilian had approached was a garden laid out in a style

long past, with box-edged borders, holly trees clipped into a variety of odd representations of animals and even birds. Sir George Fabyn would have no alteration here, and, save that it was kept in perfect order, the dead, had they looked upon it, would have recognized but little change. The old sun-dial stood on the same stone pedestal, and the carp and perch sported in the fish pond overhung with limes, in the cool green shade of which many a whispered word of love had been spoken by haughty, slippered dame and ar-moured knight, and the tale was still told of how a certain Geoffrey de Fabyne, in a torrent of passion, had flung his rival bodily into the depths of the pool, from which he had never risen, and even now his spectral form haunted the place, and at certain seasons was plainly visible to those who had the hardihood to venture near a spot so gruesome. Such was the story which the oldest gossips in Sidcombe firmly believed in, and loved to relate over the glowing embers when the bolts and bars were secured, and they sipped their stiff brew of hot whisky toddy and listened to the roar of the gale and the boom of the wind-tossed waves. Such was The Towers, and Lilian Fabyn treasured up and firmly believed in every one of the romantic traditions relating to her home, with all a young girl's love of the vanished years of chivalry and knighthood. Sir George Fabyn's portly figure blocked the main entrance; the very picture of an English country squire he looked, with a jolly, good-natured face and a smile and a jest for every one; deep chested and strong of limb, and despite his weight, liking nothing better than a run with the hounds, or a hard day over the turnips; and the partridge had to be a cunning old bird that escaped the deadly right and left of his double-barrelled breech-loader.

"Why, Lilian, my girl, you've only just time to dress," were the words he greeted her with as he saw her coming towards him. "Ledsham dines with us, Bolton too, and the rector."

"Not late, father dear, I hope."

"No, no, you jade, we shouldn't have begun without you. But what is that under your arm? Where have you been?"

"Sketching, or rather, trying to. But I had to save Rex from a watery grave, so have not finished it."

"You will find some parcels waiting for your inspection inside," he answered, not noticing her remark. "How well you are looking, little woman, and such a colour," he added, as he slipped his arm fondly round his daughter's waist, and drew her towards him. If there was one thing on earth he loved with all the strength of his big, manly heart it was his child, his only one.

"Am I, father? Then give me a kiss and let me go, or I shall be terribly behind, and keep you all waiting," answered Lilian, with a laugh, and holding up her lips playfully.

"God bless you, my darling," he said, as he pressed them fondly with his grizzled moustache. "Now I won't keep you any longer," he added, as he relinquished his hold, and stood to watch her graceful figure as she tripped light as a fairy up the polished oak staircase. " So beautiful, so beautiful," he muttered to himself, more slowly following her. " No wonder that she takes them all by storm. Underwood's hard hit, I could read it in his face, and Ledsham too, or why should he drop in so often, and yet, she'll have none of them. That's as it should be. Why should she be snatched away, the very joy of my life? and besides she is too young. But yet I am sure I am right. There's more in it than I know. She's not happy, not happy. God help her. And so young. But I must try to get at the root of the matter. She can't deceive me." Talking thus to himself, Sir George entered his dressing-room and shut the door. Within the hour, a very well-cooked and well-served dinner was being discussed in the dining-room at The Towers. The table was decorated with a tasteful profusion of hot-house flowers, shining silver-plate, and an enormous wine cooler reposed in a convenient position, filled with a cosy

array of long-necked bottles. Lady Fabyn
sat at the lower end, facing her husband.
She was a large, showily dressed woman,
who, but for a certain mean expression,
imparted to her face by her mouth, the lips
of which were singularly thin and met like
the two edges of a vice, might have still been
termed handsome. On her right sat the
rector, an affable white-haired man of sixty
or thereabouts. The seat on her left hand
was occupied by the Honourable James
Ledsham, or Jim Ledsham as he was more
familiarly known. Lilian Fabyn sat next to
him. And a neighbouring squire, by name,
Richard Bolton, of Bolton Hall, was seated
opposite. The Honourable Jim was going
the pace, if one might be allowed to judge
him by the soft glances which he shot from
the depths of his greenish eyes, and the
well-turned compliments and pretty nothings
he stooped to whisper in Lilian's ear. His
social status not unnaturally made him consider himself of sufficiently high standing
to enable him to aspire to the hand of any

woman in the county. And in the present case he had good reason to suppose that he was regarded in not an unfavourable light by at least one person present, whose consent would be an essential feature in the negotiations which he contemplated. Liveried servants glided noiselessly round, attending with pompous assiduity, snapping up a half-emptied glass here, and whipping up the choice and not nearly demolished contents of a plate there, with all the vigour and pertinacity not uncommon to their class. The good-natured but prosy old rector, Mr. Laxby Randal, related a few clerical anecdotes carefully selected from his not too well furnished store, and Squire Bolton and Sir George kept up a running fire, in which local topics, the county packs, and the attitude of the government during the existing crisis, mainly figured. Lilian looked just the least bit bored, and, the first moment she could, obeyed her mother's signal, leaving the gentlemen to the enjoyment of certain vintages of age and rare bouquet, glad to retire to the drawing-room, and avail herself of the few moments of respite which it gave her. But she was doomed to disappointment, and was roused from a brief reverie into which she had fallen by the sound of Lady Fabyn's voice.

" Lilian."

" Yes, mother."

" Mr. Ledsham seems to admire you immensely." Lady Fabyn was fishing, and what she lacked in skilfulness and tact, she certainly did not atone for by the harsh tone of voice in which she spoke.

" He does me too much honour, mother."

" Nonsense ; don't be stupid, child ; he could scarcely do that ; you are our child."

" Well, it is very good of him."

" How ridiculously you talk ! But he is rich. Breakwood is a charming place, don't you think so ? He will be Lord Goddington at no very distant date. I am told that the health of the old lord has not improved of late. He has gone to Cannes by the advice of the doctors, who consider his condition a most critical one, and——

" Well, mother."

" It is not every young man's luck in life to come in for a rent roll such as he will inherit."

Lilian had been listlessly turning over the pages of some new music, and she was about to try a waltz, the music of which, as she skimmed it over, she thought rather pretty, when the nature and pointed persistency of her mother's remarks dawned upon her mind. She swung round on the music stool and confronted her with an expression of wonderment and inquiry on her face which Lady Fabyn was not slow to read; but she folded her hands demurely, as if well satisfied so far with the part that she had played.

" I am very sorry about Lord Goddington, mother; of course he has been ill for months. But how can either his death or Mr. Ledsham's accession to the title possibly concern me? "

" Very much."

" What *do* you mean? "

Lady Fabyn rose from her seat, deposited on a table the copy of Tennyson, which she had nervously picked up, and coming close to her daughter's side, placed her arm round her neck. "Lilian, it has been the wish of my heart, dear, latterly, and I am convinced from what I witnessed to-night, that you have it in your power to marry quite the catch of the season. I mean "—and here she became visibly agitated—" to become Lady Goddington."

"Then I am sure I never shall be," broke from Lilian's lips.

Lady Fabyn's manner changed; she had not looked for such determined language from her daughter, gentle and flexible as a child up to this hour of her life; she regretted now that she had spoken, that she had not allowed events to take their own course. Why had she committed so ill-advised a blunder? It was a mistake, and already she began to rue it; but her reasoning, like all regrets, came too late. There was nothing for it now but to face the storm she had created, to quell and reduce it to submission by the stern assertion of her authority and influence.

She was equal to the occasion, and as her lips closed tightly, she laid her hand once more on her daughter's arm, and drew herself to her full height, like Lady Capulet, determined that cost what it might her daughter should bend to her will, and do her bidding.

"Lilian." The sound of her own name recalled her thoughts from thinking of the man she loved, so far away, and now so utterly unable to help her. Besides he did not care for her; that was the bitter thought; that was the gall and wormwood which entered into her very soul, keen as the stab of a knife, subtle as the poison of asps. Her face was bloodless, blanched as marble, pitiful to look upon, and Lady Fabyn read its meaning at a glance.

"Mother, to pursue this subject further is useless. I do not love the man and *I never shall.*" With a choking sob, which she could not restrain, she broke from Lady Fabyn's grasp and fled from the room. Once alone with herself, she buried her face and moaned aloud, stretched full length on her bed ; and her whole frame shook with a convulsive torrent of anguish. Pale moonbeams streamed through the window, and shed their calm, cold light upon her. Silent witnesses of her misery. They only and God.

CHAPTER V.

"AND your son Gerald, Mrs. Clarencourt. Is he well?"

"My dear Lady Fitzwilliam, I believe he is. He has a capital constitution, you know, and never suffered from any severe illness in his life. But I seldom hear from him."

"How is that?" asked her listener, somewhat curiously, and presuming upon her long friendship with Mrs. Clarencourt. A friendship extending over many years, but which, strange to say, had never enabled her to see into or understand Mrs. Clarencourt's character one bit better than she had done a week after their acquaintance had commenced, though they had driven together, sat in the same box at the opera and theatre, and met scores of times at the houses of mutual

friends. For they both belonged to the same
set. Once and once only had Lady Fitzwilliam
been invited to partake of the hospitality of
Clifford's Wood.

"I cannot tell you. He is in India at
present, I don't quite know where. Calcutta,
I think. At least he sailed for that port. He
wished to go alone, but, of course, that was
not to be thought of for a moment. I in-
sisted upon Wilson accompanying him. You
remember Wilson. A very old and valued
servant of my poor dear husband." Mrs.
Clarencourt pronounced the last three words in
the correct stereotyped form. She turned her
head slightly so that Lady Fitzwilliam should
not see her face, and lowering her voice until
it almost sank into a whisper, gazed dreamily
into vacancy, as if conjuring before her
visions of his dear face and form. The cur-
tain has risen, but the scene to make it intelligible must be explained. It was merely
Mrs. Clarencourt's drawing-room, in a small
house, rented by her annually, situated in one
of the side streets opening into Park Lane,

and the two ladies were indulging in a cup of orange pekoe to aid them in their friendly chat. Lady Fitzwilliam in appearance was like scores of other women to be met with in every day life, a face possessing nothing in it to give you reason for dislike, rather the reverse; but not sufficiently striking in any way to cause you to remember its existence five minutes after having talked to her. Well-dressed and fashionable looking. There the description must end for fault of a subject. Mrs. Clarencourt was worthy of closer attention. Her figure was that of a splendidly preserved middle-aged woman of something over forty, though she would have passed for at least ten years younger, with light hair, pale blue eyes, and sharply defined features. It was her mouth alone which betrayed her, and imparted to her whole face that cold, heartless expression with which it was habitually stamped. Haughty and domineering, but without one vestige of love, save for herself, in her whole composition. Vain of her personal attractions, inordinately vain of her own family connections and what she chose to consider stainless pedigree. Such was a rough outline of Gerard Clarencourt's mother, and what wonder that he sought her love and failed to win it? Had he climbed to a higher sphere, and occupied, perhaps, some prominent Government appointment, gratified pride would have prompted her to consider him worthy of her notice. As it was she considered him rather a bore, and was pleased enough that he had taken himself abroad. His presence made her feel old, and, what was worse still, look it; her vanity was piqued at sight of him, and to have had a great big strapping fellow of his age calling himself her son, and constantly living with her, would have the very reverse of a favourable impression upon the men with whom she deigned to flirt. Yet that was not the *only* reason for her unnatural dislike of him.

"Men are so dilatory. They never seem to think of others in the very least. I might worry myself until I grew positively thin with anxiety about him yet he would not

trouble himself to write a few lines to
me."

"Really; I am so surprised. He seemed
such an amiable lad, as I remember him,"
replied Lady Fitzwilliam.

"That was years ago, when he was only a
tiny urchin."

"True, so it was."

"Ah, things are changed now. Though
he is very young, quite a boy, I assure
you, still he is old enough to be trouble-
some if his will is thwarted in the very
least degree, and, poor, dear lad, I thought
a good long voyage might have a beneficial
effect upon him. Nothing like an intimate
knowledge of other countries and modes of
life for enlarging the mind, and then people
do say that one never does appreciate home
ties thoroughly until they have been severed
for a time, and so I am tempted to hope
that he will come back quite a changed
child." Mrs. Clarencourt might have been
talking of an infant of ten instead of a
strong, handsome fellow something over

twenty, but she smiled and simpered, and
told her little grievances with such an
outward semblance of truth that Lady
Fitzwilliam was almost gulled into believing
Gerard one of the most refractory of sons.
But there was one point upon which she
could not refrain from laughing in her
sleeve, and that was the cool way in which
Mrs. Clarencourt talked of her *child*.
Lady Fitzwilliam was, however, far too
politic to pass any remark, or to venture
upon any inquiries, knowing, as she did,
Mrs. Clarencourt's age, to a year or so, at
any rate. The furniture and ornaments
in the apartment were luxurious in the
extreme, presenting tangible proofs of a
well-plenished exchequer. Rare and fragrant
hot-house plants, grown in costly majolica
vases, mirrors in Dresden, representing
laughing, rosy-cheeked cupids, surrounded
by imaginative bowers of flowers in full
bloom. Tastefully executed water-colours,
by some of the first men of the day,
adorned the walls, and the light was

excluded from the room at will by pale tinted silk blinds, edged with deep lace, and soft-hued curtains of rich stuffs. Half a dozen white bear and magnificent tiger skins were strewn on the long-piled Turkey carpet, on which no footfall could be heard. It was essentially the home of a lady of refined taste, for such Mrs. Clarencourt undoubtedly was, and months yearly spent upon the Continent, added to her knowledge on the subject, had enabled her to fill her cabinets with miracles of art, old, and of a value which would have made many a London dealer envious. Lady Fitzwilliam accepted the offer of another cup of tea and a wafer, which she nibbled slowly, and she was about to bid her friend good-bye, with the addition of an affectionate kiss, when she remembered the object of her visit.

"Dear me, I have such a bad memory. Would you believe it? I was nearly forgetting something most important."

"What was it, dear?" asked Mrs. Clarencourt.

" Are you engaged for Thursday next ? "

" No, I think not."

" Well, it is a very short notice, but we have known each other so long, and I thought I would just come and ask you myself to dine with us on that day."

" Thanks, but——"

" I shall take no refusal, my dear ; we are going to the opera afterwards, and Colonel Cheston has promised to come." Lady Fitzwilliam was particularly anxious for reasons of her own to secure Mrs. Clarencourt's society, so she threw out her last bait, and watched its effect. Of late, Colonel Cheston's name had often been mentioned in connection with the fair widow's, and certain circumstances had occurred which had given rise to no small amount of gossip. It had the desired effect. Mrs. Clarencourt expressed her pleasure, and accepted the invitation. Having gained her point, Lady Fitzwilliam drove away, delighted with herself and her success. The great aim in Mrs. Clarencourt's life had been to possess wealth, and even in her

young days she had never permitted morbid
sentiment to assert its sway. Where gold
and love hung evenly in the scales before her
she had scorned, as a piece of maudlin hum-
bug, the latter; it could not last, she had
schooled herself to think, and why should
she fool away her life and choose it? She
had seen the evil of it once, in the case of
her own parents, and that one instance was
enough. The saying that when poverty stalks
in at the door, love flies out at the window,
she firmly believed in, and naturally enough,
with such a belief, her faith in the durability
of the softer passion was weak indeed. What
wonder, then, that she, the youngest daughter
of an impoverished Irish gentleman, whose
stainless descent from old and honourable
families was well nigh all he had to cling to,
seized the first opportunity which offered,
and married, wholly and solely for his money,
Mr. Clarencourt, Gerard's father, who had
fallen madly in love with her, and proposed,
a few weeks after they first met, in a crowded
ball-room at Dublin? Thus, she had sealed

her own fate and his. He had not been slow to discover that the woman he had married had grossly deceived him, although she had striven to hide her real feelings cleverly, and had glossed over many palpable neglects in word and deed with all an ingenious woman's skilful tact. Still, she could not hide from him the fact that she did not love him. They had lived together in a very prosaic, matter-of-fact way, never interfering with each other, and to all outward appearances they continued to present a spotless front to the world's criticisms. Even the birth of Gerard did not unite them; to all intents and purposes they remained as far apart as ever, and the single word which lay at the root of the matter, small and insignificant in itself, but possessing a terrible meaning to him, had he learnt it, was *envy*. He had given her his love and a beautiful home. All that his wealth could procure had been lavished upon her, and its only effect had been to cause her to hate him yet the more. Most women would have felt

content, once their ends gained, their
ambition satisfied ; not so with her. She
envied him the absolute possession of the
money. Why should it be in his power to
do so much, and in hers so little ? Should
she stoop and cringe to him ? The feeling
was there, and it had slumbered and rankled
in her heart, but never for a moment died
out. Again she had her will. After a
lingering illness he had died, and as she
knew that he loved her to the last, she felt
sure that he would leave his wealth to her,
or at least by far the greater portion. When
the will was read she had stifled her indignation under a calm exterior ; but it was
there none the less. She was told that the
money and estates would be hers until her
son attained the age of twenty-five, after which
time they would pass to him, with the exception of an annuity of one thousand per annum.
Should he fail to live to that age, everything
which had belonged to the deceased was vested
in her during her life, and afterwards would
pass away to a distant branch of the Clarencourt

family. From the date of the reading of that will the feeling of dislike had been transferred from father to son. This it was which had caused her to banish him from her presence on any available pretence. When with her the sounds of his boyish laughter grated upon her ear. She regarded her own flesh and blood in the light of an usurper, and smilingly as she had conversed about him with Lady Fitzwilliam, had concealed all her real thoughts and feelings with the consummate tact of which she was mistress. Her guest departed, Mrs. Clarencourt summoned her maid, and resigned herself into her hands to be dressed prior to making her appearance at a fashionable *réunion* at which she had been bidden to attend. No thought of her son entered into her head; she had dismissed him from her mind an hour after Lady Fitzwilliam left, though for that brief period she had wondered not a little what motive had prompted that good lady's curiosity. But determined to enjoy herself, callous of how he fared, she entered her brougham, arrayed in an elegant toilette, proud and serene, and all the more so because she felt that Élise had done her hair to perfection, and that she was looking her best.

CHAPTER VI.

"NO MAN SHALL ROB ME OF YOU AND LIVE."

SEVERAL weeks had passed, and still Gerard
Clarencourt lingered in Calcutta. Weeks,
which had fled only too fast for him, for they
were made up of days of unalloyed happiness.
Still he stayed on, as regardless of the heat
as he was of the object of his visit to India.
What cared he now for Delhi, Lucknow, and
Cawnpore? All the visions which his strong
imagination had pictured of their gorgeous
Eastern magnificence and historical fame had
long deserted him. If he ever thought at all
on the subject, he must have told himself that
they would keep until he had spare time at
his disposal in which to visit them. Spare
time, what a farce it was! why he had literally
nothing to do, nothing on which to turn his
attention, from the moment he rose in the early

morning until night, when he was forced to retire because everybody else did so—nothing, save to dream, to think of, and sometimes to see Ada Devereaux. She knew full well how to handle one so hot tempered and impetuous as Gerard; she read and understood his character, or thought she did, which came to the same thing, so judged it advisable to keep him in an agony of suspense, by hiding the light of her presence from him for a whole day or so, during which period Gerard would fret and fume, and wander listlessly about the place as if he had not a single aim or object in life worth living for, save her. This was precisely the case now; he had not seen her since the day before, when in the early morning they had ridden together and she had charmed him, with the frankness of her smile, her bursts of merry laughter, and fresh healthy complexion, of which thanks to her splendid constitution even the hot Indian climate had failed to rob her. And then her horse had bucked vigorously, and tried to bolt, and she had sat him and curbed his fiery temper, reducing him to docile obedience, in a way which had called for Gerard's highest admiration, and left no doubt in his mind that riding was another accomplishment in which she excelled. Poor Gerard, securely was he caught within the toils of her witchery. The sun had risen amid all the bright-hued tinting of clouds and brilliant colouring of a daybreak in the East. Down by the banks of the river, under the heavy arching foliage, groups of natives chatted and laughed, fruit and sweetmeat sellers, with tough-looking visages the colour of musty parchment, displayed their wares on low wooden stalls, or squatted on a square of matting *à la turque*, sat with their goods piled round them, anxiously awaiting the appearance of their first customer, who their religious superstition forbade to send away empty-handed, or without having concluded the bargain, no matter what the sum offered to them. Dealers in curiosities of quaint and pretty workmanship. Women of every age, children and active lithe-limbed girls, their full lips dyed red

with the juice of the betel nut they loved to
chew, and others older still, in the prime of
life, according to a European's ideas on age,
but already wofully wrinkled and possessing
stumps black as ebony in place of even
shining rows of teeth. Old hags stooping on
the hard mud which the tide had left exposed
to view, to mould their earthen bowls and
water vessels, soon to become hardened by the
scorching sunlight. Many chattering strings
of coolies sang their incessant monotonous
chants as they laboured on the decks of the
merchant sailing ships, for the business of the
day had commenced for them too. Swarms
of dingies were moored to the mud banks,
or swiftly darted in and out midst the crowd-
ing hulls of the vessels, sculled by their bony-
limbed, brown-skinned owners, laden with fruit
and fish, meat, articles of clothing, and a
thousand other things. Bengal native infantry
men, clad in their undress uniform, hurried
along the Esplanade side by side with solemn
looking Hindoos, white turbaned and sleek
with good living. All was bustle, excited

activity and teeming life. In the bazaars and markets, business was going on briskly, and crowds of half-nude, coppery-coloured men and thinly-clad women jostled each other. Inside a shop tenanted by a jeweller stood Gerard Clarencourt; he had strolled in more from curiosity than any other motive, but his entrance had been the signal for a general pulling down of cases and display of hidden gems; miracles of art to judge by the care with which they were handled. The owner of all these treasures was seated on a pile of cushions and never stirred himself, but gravely received the goods he ordered to be brought from the hands of a lad. His face was a study worthy of Murillo, so bronzed and savage-looking was it in expression, with features of a slightly Jewish type, and keen, piercing, deep-set eyes, which scowled wickedly upon Gerard when he was not looking, and the place was reeking with the stale smell of the smoke which he blew in great clouds from his hubble-bubble. Nothing had especially pleased Gerard's

fancy, when the man, thinking that perhaps he had underrated the length of his
visitor's purse, produced a set of delicate
champac ornaments of exquisitely fine workmanship, and made of dull red gold. The
man's eyes gleamed even more hideously with
avarice. He read the look on Gerard's face
as he inspected the jewellery, and mentally
determining that in the English sahib he had
secured a certain customer, raised the original
price to a ruinous extent and sat silently
waiting for him to speak.

"How much are they?" asked Gerard
carelessly.

"Five hundred rupees, sahib," answered
the fellow, in intelligible English.

"Absurd! You are trying to rob me."

"My God all same your God, sahib. I
not lie; I no rob you." But his brief sojourn
in Calcutta had taught Gerard a lesson, and,
as he was not to be swindled with impunity,
he took out a pocket-book, mentally perform-
ing a small calculation in arithmetic as he
did so.

"I shall give you one-third of the sum you ask." The man hummed and hawed, swore he would be ruined, and went through a little pantomime of his own, which ended as Gerard handed him the money and left the bazaar with the champac ornaments in his breast-pocket. He knew the mail from England had arrived the night before, so he strolled off in the direction of the post-office, and inquired if there were any letters for him. Three were given to him, and eagerly he turned them over, and scanned the post-marks and the handwriting. They were all from England, but none—none from his mother! His face clouded over, and the veins in his forehead stood out like cords with the agitation he felt; but it was only momentary, and passed, giving way to an expression of sorrow and gloom as he turned on his heel and left the building. What had he done to be treated thus? Plenty of time had elapsed for her to write, and yet not a line had come from her —his only near relative on earth. Why did she pass him by persistently, making him feel his loneliness and isolation so bitterly? An orphan, although his mother lived! Estranged from her—without the pale of her love, although his heart yearned towards her still, and the answer came to him and rang in his ears:

"She does not—cannot care for you; why trouble yourself about one in whose thoughts you have no place?" Slowly he took his way, as if not caring where he went, so that he might be alone with his own sad thoughts. Here was the young, untrained mind, as yet not schooled to bear the world's harshness; here was the man beginning life with fair and unclouded, prospects—without a wish which he could not satisfy—his most fastidious tastes and extravagant desires could all be gratified. He had but to express a want, and straightway, as in the old fable of the "Arabian Nights," he had it. Lucky dog! Those who knew the outside shell of his life would have said, "What can he lack more?" And yet Gerard Clarencourt had his trouble—his one great gnawing source

of unhappiness; and from the day he began
to think, and turn his attention from his
infant toys, he felt it, and in secret bore the
sorrow and the pain of the canker which had
eaten into his childish happiness, his boyish
pleasures, and now his manhood's hopes and
ambitions. He had nothing—no one to live
for. There was a blank in his life—an empty
void, which could only be filled up in one
way. Oddly enough, his steps had wandered
along the wide street which led past Government House, and he found himself near to
the upper end of the Gardens. It wanted
hours until he had any actual engagement—
until he should see her. So he opened the
wicket-gate, and stood under the thick, tropical foliage, and watched the bushy-tailed, grey
squirrels as he paced down one of the leafy
avenues which led to the painted Burmese
pagoda where he had first met her. Mrs.
Devereaux had plunged into her bath, dressed,
or rather suffered herself to be attired in a
charming morning toilette, and had sipped
her coffee, with the great, swinging folds of

the punkah ceaselessly sending its rush of air
across her white forehead, lifting the wavy
curls from off it as it played amidst her hair.
The old punkah-wallah was sound asleep, or
appeared to be so, for he performed his func-
tions with eyes closed and his head sunk upon
his chest, occasionally giving vent to a low,
guttural grunt as he tugged at the string
which moved the monster fan. In through
the windows came the sweet scent of Cape
jasmine, and a thousand other fragrant
odours, from the gardens outside. Mrs.
Devereaux seemed thoroughly discontented
and annoyed with herself—an unenviable
state of mind truly, but it was none the less
perfectly apparent. She drummed with her
foot upon the floor, stirred the liquid in her
cup angrily, thereby spilling some of the
contents, beat a tattoo with her knife, for
the second time scanned the addresses of
some letters placed for her perusal, and then,
with evident impatience, cut them open one
by one, and threw them aside with varied
remarks on their several contents. It was

not often that Mrs. Devereaux condescended or humbled herself to such an extent as to show any irritability or spleen from which she chanced to be suffering to the outside world. She was too consummate a mistress of herself, and would have regarded an ebullition of temper from the same standpoint, and with the same satire, that she would have used in discoursing upon inebriety in any person who happened to come under her notice. A man never shows to less advantage than when he is intoxicated; then all his worst points are revealed, and he is powerless to hide them. He is a fool when he thus places himself at the mercy of others. She had once said this; and much in the same way she argued that to show your hand was to discover your own weakness, and was tantamount to surrendering all chance of the game—no matter what the mask hid, so long as it served the purpose of a complete disguise, and was never for a moment removed. What had upset her equilibrium? That was a question far too difficult to solve. Perhaps

the fit of some dress had displeased her, or
her maid had clumsily performed her duties.
She was put out—that was enough, and the
servants knew it, and, as they glided noiselessly about the house, took very good care
to give their mistress as wide a berth as they
conveniently could. At length she settled
herself before her davenport, wrote several
letters in answer to the ones she had received,
tidied some bundles of papers, and finally
subsided into a sofa, scanning over the
pages of the latest novel she had been able
to procure until it wanted scarce half an
hour to tiffin. A servant entered the room;
it was her maid.

"A gentleman wishes to see you, madam,"
said the woman, who was French, but could
speak English tolerably well.

"What an insufferable nuisance!" replied
Mrs. Devereaux, as she raised herself slightly
on her elbow. "Just as I was beginning to
get interested too. Who is he? Did he give
his name?"

"I do not know, madam. I did not see the

gentleman, but I will inquire. Mr. Carelesse, madam," continued the woman, as she returned with the required information.

"Very well, show him up, but remember, I am not at home to any one else until evening." Mrs. Devereaux rose from the sofa, arranged her hair to her entire satisfaction before a mirror, and turned round just as Carelesse entered the room. The expression of his face told her in a moment that something unexpected had occurred. She could almost divine the truth at a glance, but whatever she had discovered, it pleased her.

"You are surprised to see me here so early," he said, after he had taken her hand in his and sat down in a chair.

"Surprised, but none the less pleased." How well she could dissemble! How easy it was to her to meet his eyes, and tell him of her pleasure at seeing him, when in her heart she wished the man anywhere, a thousand miles removed from her; dead, if need be, rather than where he was!

"Thanks; but I come on a sorry errand.

I suppose I should be glad, but I am not."

"Why, what do you mean? Come, Geoffrey, don't look so down-hearted. Tell me what has happened to disturb the even tenor of your life."

The sound of his Christian name uttered by her made him raise his head.

"Can you not guess?"

"No, how should I? Nothing more awful than that you have lost some money at pool, or made some rash bet with Captain Garrick, and found that it is possible to lose; or is it anything infinitely more distressing?" She gave vent to one of her low, rippling laughs, but the sound he loved to hear at times grated harshly on his ear now. It was painfully out of place to him. Yet, how should she know? he thought. It never struck him that the present state of affairs as set forth by the daily papers might furnish her with a clue, and added to that that she could read every passing change on his face like the pages of a book she had learnt by heart.

" Ada, you jest, and at such a time ! "

" If you are not altogether unreasonable, you will explain yourself."

She was dying to hear, to have her suspicions confirmed, and her pulse beat considerably faster as she leant back amongst her cushions, and looked at him with her blue eyes sparkling with the light that she could call into them and slay with at will. But not one trace of eagerness to learn the object of his visit was discernible in her manner.

" I—I shall have to leave you soon, dear," at length he said, his voice thick with the emotion he could not restrain.

" Geoffrey, please do explain yourself." Had he not been so pre-occupied and so thoroughly out of spirits, even he could not have failed to recognize a faint tinge of exultation in the ringing mellowness of her voice. " So long as it pleases you to make use of enigmas you cannot possibly expect me to grasp your meaning. Let me know the worst."

" Ada, we are ordered to the front at last."

" What fearfully sudden news ! "

" Well, I don't know, my darling." He had
taken her soft, plump hand in his. " We have
been expecting the order for weeks."

So had she, and had dreamed of the possible chance of escape from him that would
be hers in case of such a contingency.

" But I said nothing to you," he continued,
" as I had hoped that it would not come to
this. Of course you know as we all do that
the Russians are encroaching on the frontiers
of Afghanistan, and the Ameer is massing
his troops to hold them in check. An open
rupture is hourly feared. We are support-
ing the Afghans, and shall do so, I hope,
through thick and thin, and any available
troops that can be mustered are ordered to
the up country stations *en route* for the front.
We are amongst the number." Many soft
words of endearment she addressed to him
in reply, until Carelesse began to hope that
it was not so bad after all, that it would
give him his chance of promotion which he
had so longed for before he had met her,

and that his dreams as he had had them
when on board the huge troopship, full of
zeal for the service he had entered, would
be realized—dreams which had made him
long for a smart campaign, a heavy brush
with the Ruskies, in which of course he was
to come off scot free with the V.C. How
his young heart had burned to do something
great! Full of hope, without a care, he
had passed and was actually gazetted to a
regiment. What a different being he was
now, now that this woman had crossed his
path! As the weaker mind must inevitably
succumb and become subservient to the
stronger if thrown into close and constant
intercourse, so had Geoffrey Carelesse bowed
before the strength of will, and what he
recognized as the superior ability of
Mrs. Devereaux, but what was in reality
merely a greater knowledge of the world,
aided by personal beauty, and powers of
finesse added to the subtilty and arts of
a beautiful woman. He was passionately
in love, while she was not; he believed

in, and was ready to obey her slightest word, her most imperious behest, whilst she listened to all he chose to say with an ear only tuned to catch at and store to advantage the words which might place him more securely in her power. The contest was very uneven. The game was in her hands, and she knew it. Such power had she been able to exert over Carelesse, that two or three days after the stormy interview in which he had proved his knowledge of at least some portion of her past life, and had accused her of playing fast and loose with him and encouraging Clarencourt, she had entirely dispelled any such ideas from his mind, flouted him with being envious of such a mere boy, to use his own words, and then put on a deeply offended air, and wondered how he *could* think so ill of her as to accuse her of being guilty of such treachery. So skilfully did she' mislead him, that Carelesse, easily duped and worse than blind to *her* faults, had been forced to acknowledge himself in the wrong and had sued for her forgiveness, which she granted him with one of her seductive smiles, but only upon one condition. Carelesse would do anything for her sake. Very well; he should himself carry a note of invitation from her to Gerard Clarencourt and should meet him as her guest under her roof. To all of which propositions he had agreed, and the two men had consequently met several times in this way.

"Ada," Carelesse continued after his brief explanation of the reason for their sudden departure; "you know well what I would ask of you were I in the position to do so, but you would not, you could not think better of me if I broached such a subject placed as I am. I must do my duty now, and then when we meet again perhaps I shall have gained one step at least in rank. If we do come to blows with the Russians there will be plenty of casualties in our ranks, and I shall have all the more chance, unless some stray bullet does happen to find its billet in me."

" Don't say such horrible things, Geoffrey."

" Why, you know such a thing might happen; and if—if it did," he added with a sickly attempt at a smile, " I would ask you to think kindly of me, Ada."

" Of course I should ; but, oh, Geoffrey ! how can you speak so! is this likely to cheer me ? "

" Well, forgive me ; but one can't help feeling a bit melancholy sometimes."

" Nonsense, you mustn't talk so stupidly. When do you go ? "

" We shall be on the march within forty-eight hours."

" So soon? " she asked in a low voice, which vibrated and trembled with cleverly assumed pathos.

" It is too true, Ada. Our orders are to quit here with as little delay as possible. Have you seen Steele ? "

" Not as yet. How can you ask me? had he been here he would have told me the news, but he will be sure to turn up soon."

" Yes, confound him, I suppose he will ;

like his infernal impudence." A savage light gleamed in Carelesse's eyes as he spoke, which too plainly showed that, on his side at all events, no friendly feeling existed towards his colonel and superior officer .

"How absurd of you, Geoffrey ; why, really it is too ridiculous. Only the other day you were frightfully jealous of Mr. Clarencourt, and now poor Colonel Steele has been luckless enough to incur your displeasure."

"Oh, deuce take him ! I should like to punch his head. I know he tries to spoon you, Ada, and it makes me wild to think of it ; besides, apart from that, there is no love lost between us. He dislikes me, and I'll swear I hate him."

"Fie, Geoffrey, I really am ashamed of you. To speak in this strain of your commanding officer ; it is nothing short of rank mutiny. I think I must take it upon me to report you."

"Don't tease me, Ada, that's all. But I do detest Steele," answered Carelesse, with a poor attempt at a laugh. During the whole

of the conversation, the moment after Carelesse had announced the sudden departure of
the regiment, Mrs. Devereaux's brain had
been at work; she had been revolving certain
little projects of which she had had but
dim visions before the conversation, as she
had not permitted her mind to dwell upon
a hope which had presented itself to her
as a kind of chimera, not to be entertained
because it was delusive and, on the whole, too
good to be true. But now, since it had
turned out to be a reality, it was worthy of
her careful consideration. While he had remained in Calcutta she could not leave it without the risk of offending him, which risk she
dare not run. She judged Carelesse harshly,
and had told herself that if a quarrel ensued
between them he would instantly be revenged
upon her by maligning her to mutual friends.
Never had she formed a more erroneous
opinion. Whatever were his faults, and they
were many, meanness did not figure upon the
list. He was capable of shooting her dead
where she stood if she played him false, but

never of resorting to slander as an outlet for
his vengeance. He was passionate and vin-
dictive; but never base and sordid. Yes,
this was without doubt the chance of which
she must avail herself if she wished to place
a safe distance between her own person
and that of Geoffrey Carelesse. What better
opportunity could have occurred? He was
ordered up country on active service. She
would return to England, and that without
awakening his suspicions in the very least.
What more natural than that she should wish
to rejoin her friends now that he was thus
roughly snatched from her? The ideas dove-
tailed to a nicety. No sooner had she
sketched the outline in her mind than she
determined to tell him of its existence.

"When *shall* we meet again, Ada?" he said
tenderly as he leant over her. This was the
key-note she needed. It would aid her to
make the revelation she meditated.

"Why, when you return to England, dear."

"England, Ada; what are you thinking
of?"

"Why, you don't imagine that I shall remain here after you have gone; at least, no longer than I can help. The place would be simply odious to me. And what good could it do? You may never return here at all, and are just as likely to embark for home so soon as the war is ended."

"You don't like one soul here but me, and, save for my being here, would have left long ago. My darling, how could I have been such a brute as to doubt you?"

He threw his arms round her as he spoke and pressed his lips to hers. She never attempted to repel him, but suffered him to cover her with kisses. It was part of the *rôle* she had set herself, and she was scarcely the woman to ruin her game by flinching or discovering her real feelings by displaying a want of nerve.

"Go to England, Ada; you will be safer there, and we shall meet again, never doubt it. I love you as no other man ever can. Be true to me, my darling, and all will yet be well. But, Ada, I call God to witness my

oath.   No man shall rob me of you and
live."

Carelesse's face was convulsed with the
emotion he was a prey to ; his voice was un-
steady and thick. He managed to tell her
that he should see her again before he left Calcutta, and then, as if afraid to trust himself
in her presence longer, hurriedly quitted the
room. When they next met it was a terrible
meeting to both of them, and in the interval,
that wild oath, flung out as if challenging
God and man, rung in Mrs. Devereaux's ears :
" No man shall rob me of you and live."

CHAPTER VII.

WHY NOT RETURN?

On the evening of the same day on which
Geoffrey Carelesse had told of the sudden
departure of his regiment for the front, Mrs.
Devereaux's drawing-room was tenanted by
another visitor, and this time it was Gerard
himself. He had returned to his hotel after
having sauntered aimlessly about the Gardens
in the early morning, and had spent the time
which intervened before nightfall pretty
equally between the pages of what papers
and periodicals he could get, a new novel, an
endless consumption of cheroots, and growls
at Wilson for real or fancied clumsiness in
the performance of his duties. And so the
hours had sped, and at length Gerard, who
had looked at his watch a score of times
before, found that he could call at Mrs.

Devereaux's bungalow with something like propriety. Mrs. Devereaux had seated herself at the piano in obedience to a request from him, but her fingers strayed idly over the keys, breaking first into one air, wild and passionate, and the next moment into another, soft and pathetic. Even in that desultory way she was pleasing him; he was content to listen. Afraid of breaking the thread of her thoughts by speaking, he had left her side, and stood gazing out into the garden. Yet as she played she was thinking of him. By cautiously questioning Carelesse she had ascertained a good deal about Gerard; above all she had found out that beyond a doubt he was rich, and that was the chief point upon which she had required information. Her mind was satisfied so far; but although she fully intended to return to England, she was by no means prepared to lose sight of him, and that reason accounted for her preoccupied manner. It caused her to think, and her thoughts puzzled her not a little. She knew that she already possessed some influence over him, the amount of which she rather under than over rated, though not aware of it. She had never questioned him as to his future movements, confident that he would remain in Calcutta so long as it pleased her fancy; but now her own had undergone a change it might be well to learn his intentions. No sooner had this thought dawned upon her than she ceased playing abruptly, and turned towards him.

"Mr. Clarencourt."

"Why did you stop? please go on; that air reminded me of, of——" he hesitated, as a host of recollections were forced upon him, and he would rather that his words had remained unsaid.

"Of what does it remind you, Mr. Clarencourt?" She was curious to learn the reason for his embarrassment, and as she asked the question she kept her eyes fixed upon him.

"Oh, only of my mother, it was a great favourite of hers," he replied as he recovered himself. The answer did not satisfy Mrs. Devereaux; although she did not care for him in the very least, apart from her own ends, it was that fact which made her jealous and suspicious of any person capable of influencing him. And she was not to be deceived in this instance, the awkwardness of his manner had not failed to impress her, and it told her just as plainly as words could have done that Mrs. Clarencourt, if she so pleased, might be a very dangerous foe to encounter. Inwardly she resolved to say nothing more on the subject just then, but to probe it to the bottom when a more favourable opportunity presented itself.

"Where do you intend to go after you leave Calcutta, Mr. Clarencourt?" she asked, after a short silence.

"I do not know in the very least, all places are much the same to me." There was a touch of sadness in his voice as he spoke and raised his dark blue eyes to hers inquiringly. "Why, Mrs. Devereaux? I am really too happy here to think of a change at present."

No word of love had ever crossed his

lips as yet, but he longed to tell her that she made up the sum total of his pleasures, that it was for her, for love of her, that he lingered there. He longed to know whether she did care just the least bit for him, but he mistrusted his own powers, his nerve forsook him when on the eve of an avowal, and he drew back, and shrank within himself, fearful of discovering that all his hopes were mere delusions. So beautiful and accomplished, how should she think anything more of him than of scores of other men friends? he had argued with himself. But then at times there was a something in her manner, an expression in her eyes, which caused his pulse to beat faster and his heart to throb as though it would burst, and he had tried to make himself believe that he might hope that she did love him.

"Why do you ask?" he repeated.

"Oh, simply because I am leaving here myself, and I thought it just possible that you too might be contemplating a move up country or somewhere."

"You, Mrs. Devereaux," Gerard stammered. It was such a shock to him he could scarcely frame his words. He had never once thought of the possibility of her going away.

"Yes; as soon as I can make the necessary arrangements."

"Where do you go?" he inquired, concealing his eagerness but poorly.

"Back to England. I am so funny, so eccentric in my movements," she added, "but I am getting rather tired of the heat; it tries me, and lately I have not felt quite as well as I should wish, and I think the change to the colder climate might do me good."

He was perfectly calm now. If she could speak so lightly of leaving him, of placing a few thousand miles of water between them, how could she mind one jot where he went or what became of him?

"And when do you think of sailing?" he asked in an off-hand tone, though with his lips compressed tightly and a look of

determination that she had never seen on
his face before. The coolness of the question surprised her and she glanced up at
him. It almost made her doubt her own
power for an instant. Was he really in
love with her or not? Could she be mistaken? It was impossible.

"I don't know, yet, but it will be soon.
And that reminds me, Mr. Clarencourt,
would it be too much to ask you to inquire
for me how the boats go? Of course there
are the regular mails, but there may be
others starting which would suit me equally
well; at all events it might be advisable to
know."

"I shall be delighted," he answered coolly.
"How sudden it all seems! When I was
last here I little thought that I should receive a commission from you to look out
for a steamer to convey you away. I
don't think you could have given me a
greater surprise."

Those heedless words which he spoke
tore at his very heart-strings. They hurt

him like the sharp thrusts of a stiletto.
She should not see his misery. She should
never be able to say that she had con-
quered him and won his love. No matter
what the agony he had to endure, he would
writhe under it alone, in secret, and she
should be none the wiser. Such were the
thoughts in his heart. Gerard Clarencourt
had a nature capable of loving honourably
and to desperation so long as life should
last, were the love he sought as freely given,
with a trust and frankness that equalled
his own. But the blue blood of his race
welled through his veins and his pride rescued
him from permitting his affection to be
seen where it had been misplaced. He
would have bid good-bye to Ada Devereaux
at that moment and left her with as firm
a step, and with as calm a smile upon his
face, as he would have done had the farewell, which was to separate them for ever,
been addressed to an every day acquaintance. Mrs. Devereaux, as she watched him,
began to feel anxious. She had hoped that

10—2

he would have proposed what she wished, but she saw that she had committed a blunder, though one luckily not irreparable.

"I think you said that you had no plans for the future, Mr. Clarencourt. If you have nothing better to do why not be content with what you have seen of India?"

Even yet he was obstinate, he did not choose to see what she meant.

"Then where should I go?"

"Return to England."

"With—with you?" The blood rushed to his face as the words passed his lips before he well knew that he had spoken. Mrs. Devereaux glanced at him as he said them, and that look told her that he belonged to her to do with as she chose. Then she broke into the low, sweet laugh that was so alluring and that he loved to hear.

"Yes, why not? there can be no good in your broiling yourself out here, besides it will be so nice to return together, and the voyage won't seem half so long to either of us. I shall have earned the everlasting gratitude of your relations for bringing you back."

" I have none who would care two straws whether I returned or not, or who would shed a tear the more if the next mail carried to them the news of my death."

She had struck upon a delicate chord in his being, and it had evoked that passionate reply, had aroused the demon of bitterness which lurked in the inmost recesses of his hot, impulsive nature, and the words had broken from him with the rush and impetuosity of a pent-up torrent.

" Why, you are quite cross. One would think that you had not a friend in the world to care for you, or a relation who would miss your presence. Years ago, when I was foolishly romantic, I should have been tempted to believe that you had a history ; that some blight had fallen upon your early life and had made it not quite so happy as you could have wished. I half think it now."

"Then don't, Mrs. Devereaux. The world wags with me as well as it does with others, far better than with many, I have no doubt. But few can boast that their course through it is smooth and unruffled at times by storms."

To some women it is given to console. In their faces one reads that in them exists a softness of nature, a sorrowing heart for the woes of others, a kindred spirit which soothes the troubled one, like oil upon rough waters. But to Mrs. Devereaux belonged nothing of this. That, too, was not added as a means of destruction, whereby she might the more easily have wrecked men's hearts. Many who had seen life and knew most of its ups and downs, and had learnt to value goodness as well as beauty, would have recognized this fatal defect, this lack of sympathy, and would have turned from the glamour which she shed about her unharmed, because of that blank in her character. Not so Gerard, his years had been too few to have taught him to discriminate so minutely. As he looked at her he felt that he could not confide—that he could not tell her of his inmost troubles, but he never paused or sought for a reason. It was enough for him that she was lovely as a siren.

"But you have not told me yet that you like my proposal, that you approve of it."

"With all my heart."

"And you will come, and let me tease you and drive you to distraction with endless questions, for I talk twice as much when I am at sea. The fact is, I am afraid of myself if a fit of the dumps does overtake me. From my heart I pity you, Mr. Clarencourt; I am most terribly exacting, and shall keep you half the day running for cushions and wraps, scent bottles and a thousand odds and ends. What! I have not frightened you with such a catalogue?"

"Not in the very least, nothing *could* give me more pleasure." His voice fell into a whisper, and he gazed into her eyes with the soft love light in his. He would have said more then, but she rose, with the light laugh peculiar to her. The star of brilliants which she wore in her hair scintillated under the subdued rays of the oil lamps. It was impossible for Mrs. Devereaux to move, to walk across a room without displaying an easy grace of carriage. Not the faintest trace of anything that could have been termed awkwardness by the harshest critic was ever observable in her most trifling gesture. There was that indescribable something which stamped her at once as well born and bred, no matter what her faults or the evil which lurked under that silken mask of smiles with which she cloaked her true nature. It was there, and could never be obliterated while life lasted. Gerard, as he watched her, thought to himself that before him stood the woman who would, if he won her, grace his home, of whom his father had he lived would have been proud, and against whom his mother, haughty and supercilious though she was, could scarcely cavil.

"And, with all I have said, I have not robbed myself of your allegiance?" she asked

WHY NOT RETURN? 153

in a bantering tone. Gerard answered her as
lightly :

"I am looking forward to the starting time
already."

"Then, in truth, you are a very squire of
dames, Mr. Clarencourt, if the picture of submission and patient waiting to obey my most
exacting behests which I have drawn for you
has not frightened you from taking such a
plunge."

"There is nothing that you can ask that
I will not gladly do," he answered gently.
And she knew he spoke the truth.

"Why, how stupid of me ! I have forgotten
the news of the day, which you cannot have
heard or you would have said something
before this."

"I know of none worth repeating."

"I shall tell it to you, and sing one song,
your favourite, and then you must go. I am
going to treat you quite as an old friend, and
not stand on ceremony. The news is that the
10th is ordered up country, and they leave
almost immediately. So that if you want to

see Mr. Carelesse you must go down to the
fort early to-morrow."

"I am not surprised, Mrs. Devereaux ; you
haven't been wading through long leading
articles as · I have, I expect, or you would
have wondered with me that we have not
come to blows with the Russians long ago.
They want a thrashing badly."

" Well, I am not very keen on politics, I
confess, and so Mr. Carelesse when he told me
this morning rather astonished me." She had
seated herself before the piano again while she
was speaking, and, as her voice rose and fell,
reverberating through the room to the strains
of the song he liked best to hear, he fell to
wondering whether she would care as little if
he changed places with Carelesse, and left her
for all the horrors and hardships of war.
Perhaps to fill a soldier's grave under a clump
of palms, round which had thundered the
charging squadrons in all the pomp and magnificence of war. Fighting inch by inch, and
dyeing the golden sand with the blood of
their best and bravest. A soldier's grave

with the tents of the swarming hordes of
Afghans pitched above it. Unmarked, the
rude wood cross that was once there, long
since torn up or trampled upon by the hoofs
of the Russian chargers, or the rolling wheel
of the Kebitka. Unmarked, and, alas, too
soon forgotten; chill winds and hot sultry
blasts sweeping over it and rudely stirring the
tufts of rough, coarse herbage or cactus that
had reared itself above the mouldering bones
of him that once was all that the proudest
chivalry could have wished, all that a loving
mother could have coveted. It would have
been good for Gerard had he known the
truth then, could he have learned that in
her heart of hearts she cared for him less
than for the fit of her gloves. But it was
not to be. He heard her song to the end,
thanked her, and bid her good-night with a
smile on his lips, and a tumult of happiness
within that he had never known before. Out
into the moonlit garden, he went remembering her words and teaching himself to
think that she loved him, while she watched

his retreating figure until hidden from her sight, and thought, as she moved away, what a fool he was and how easy to dupe.

CHAPTER VIII.

" DON'T do it, Mr. Gerard, don't go, sir."

The words sounded strangely like a warning to Gerard, and escaped Wilson's lips in a last appeal. He had put off the evil moment as long as he could, well knowing how impetuous his young master was, and how little likely to brook advice or interference even from him, but he dared delay no longer, and, come what might, he resolved to speak his mind fearlessly, and do his duty by the only child of his late benefactor. That morning he had received instructions to have everything packed in readiness for conveyance on board ship. Of course he had known for days that there was some probability of leaving Calcutta, but he had not been told for what destination until Gerard, in the exuberance of his joy, and in high spirits at the prospect of uncounted as well as uninterrupted golden hours to be spent with the fair Devereaux, told him that they were returning to England, and then afterwards mentioned incidentally that Mrs. Devereaux, the lady to whom he had sometimes despatched him with notes, bouquets of flowers, &c., had engaged a berth in the same steamer. It was impossible that Wilson could have been blind to the events of the past few weeks. At first he had noticed the change in Gerard's manner, and wondered what could have caused it; he was preoccupied, irritable, gloomy, or in the highest spirits, as the fit seized him, and all within the round of the clock. So different to his own even temperament, and—what caused Wilson to bestow so much thought on the matter—so changed towards himself. He could hardly recollect ever having received a harsh word from Gerard; he had been kindness and good nature itself to him until they set foot in India, and since that eventful day he had been exacting and ill-tempered, or overwhelmingly kind.

Naturally enough Wilson had not been slow
to cast about for a reason to account for
the visible change he had noticed. And
before long he became possessed with the
idea that he had discovered that cause
in the person of Mrs. Devereaux. This
suspicion became verified as small events
succeeded each other in quick succession
and by close observation he put two and
two together. It was no insolent curiosity
which actuated him, but a watchful regard
and a dread of any harm which might
come of the intimacy. From the first
moment that Wilson set eyes upon Mrs.
Devereaux might be dated a strong dislike and aversion. Inwardly, and perhaps
instinctively, he felt that she meant no good.
Gerard glanced up from the leaves of the
paper he was reading, attracted by Wilson's
words. He did not choose to recognize their
purport at first.

"What do you mean, Wilson?" he asked.

"Well, sir, if I might be bold to speak,
though I know as you'll be like to take it ill,

comin' from the likes of me. But I can't
help myself, Mr. Gerard; the truth must
out, sir, or I should bust, and never forgive
myself for not warnin' of you in time."

Gerard had thrown his head back on
the lounge on which he was reclining full
length, attired in a loose, thin-textured smoking suit. And as each word issued very
deliberately from Wilson's lips, his grey eyes,
which looked darkest blue in some lights
and almost black when the fire of his nature
was roused within him, opened their widest,
and he gazed at his servant as if he was
fully convinced that the heat of the sun had
been too much for the good man. The
whole time that he was speaking Wilson
had brushed away at a serge suit which he
was in the act of stowing into a capacious
portmanteau, with a nervous energy which
threatened to transform it speedily into something unfit for wear, if the cleansing process
continued much longer.

"Don't be doin' it, Mr. Gerard. Askin'
your pardon for saying of it, but don't you

go and let yourself be a-tempted into goin' aboard that boat with that woman."

"What the devil do you mean, Wilson?" thundered Gerard, now fairly beside himself, springing to a sitting posture, his eyes sparkling with annoyance and a red flush of anger on his cheek.

"Nothin,' sir, more than what I've said."

"I insist upon a full explanation of your extraordinary conduct."

"Well, the murder's out, Mr. Gerard, and I'm glad of it."

"What do you refer to?"

"It's just this, sir, and if it do cost me my place——"

"Are you mad, Wilson?"

"An it please you, Mr. Gerard, my mind is as clear as your own. But listen to me, sir. This thought, so sudden and unreasonable like, won't do you no good, nor nobody as belongs to you, sir, because it's all along of that woman. What did she want to go and entrap you into promisin' to go back home with her, if it was not for some purpose of her own?"

"Do you dare to speak of Mrs. Devereaux in such language?"

"It's just her and nobody else that I'm meanin'. I've watched her, sir, and she's as false as she is beautiful."

"Silence! confound you."

"No, sir; I'll just ask you for the sake of the time I've served you and yours to hear me to the end. I've not slept at nights for thinkin', and can you tell me, sir, whether I mean anythin' but what's to your good?"

"Say no more, Wilson; go about your work, and this absurd behaviour shall be passed over."

"Take warnin', Mr. Gerard, for God's sake, before it's too late. I've lived many more years than you have, sir."

"What are you afraid of? From what evil do you wish to warn me? Mrs. Devereaux is a lady, and as a friend can do me no harm."

" She's more than that to you, sir ; but it's your money she's after, and she don't care for you any more than she do for her cast-off dresses. I've seen the likes of her in my time. A lady ! you're right, sir ; there's no denyin' *that*, but false and fickle, greedy and graspin', cold as the grave, with never a thought but of how much money she'll be able to spend on her bonnets and furbelows. Wicked isn't the word for her. Didn't I see it the first time as I looked her square in face ? "

Gerard had slowly raised himself into a standing posture, the very laziness and indolence of his movements, the cold pallor of his face betokening the torrent of suppressed rage under which he laboured. He paced the room with long strides, his eyes gleaming with passionate anger, and his lithe form quivering with temper, which he could ill restrain ; but he did contrive to control himself until Wilson was apparently tired out and paused for want of breath. Then he went up to him.

" No servant, save you, should have dared to speak to me as you have done. I would have struck him down before me. Your years and faithfulness to my father shall be your plea with me. But mark what I say. Never dare to mention her name to me again. Never let it cross your lips unless with expressions of respect. The day that you do so, you leave my service. I could have borne an insult to myself, but—but *not to her.*"

One glance at the determined expression of Gerard's features had assured Wilson that his cause was hopeless. He remembered the same look in his father's face, and knew, when he saw its living impress re-awakened and stamped upon the son, that it would be as easy to divert the whirlwind from its course as to attempt to alter or dissuade him from any step which he might choose to take. Some of the old legends of the family recurred to his mind as they had been related to him, and they were believed in to the full by every labourer on the Irish estates. Of the dark, stormy and passionate Clarencourts, terrible in hate when roused by anger or jealousy, but soft and gentle as women towards those they loved and found not false. And Wilson bowed his head and murmured his last appeal.

"Mr. Gerard, forgive me, sir. I couldn't have helped what I said, no, not suppose you had killed me. I've been faithful and true to you, as I was to your father. I'm feared for you, sir, but I'll hold my peace, except to ask you to remember your mother, and do nothin' rash."

With the salt tears standing in his eyes he passed out through the door and closed it gently behind him. Through many an hour of bitter regret and misery which coiled about his heart in the years which followed Gerard had cause to remember that warning.

CHAPTER IX.

THE " SIMOOM."

THE thick brown current of the Hooghly had ceased in its upward tidal rush, and the vast volume of water was again gurgling in deep eddies on its downward course to the sea. Slowly and with majestic sweep a huge and stately steamer cleft her course into mid stream. Groups of noisy natives were watching her from under the shadow of the trees which fringed the banks; sailors paused in their work on board the liners to give her a cheer; and knots of them discussed her merits from numerous fo'castle heads and waved their hats with lusty hurrah to wish her God speed. She was barque-rigged, and painted jet black, but for the thin line of white, no broader than a narrow ribbon, which traversed her sides; her yards and the greater

portion of her masts were of the same sombre
hue, and her rigging was taut, in perfect order,
and well set up. The single word "Simoom"
caught the eye in plain letters upon her bows,
and under her counter it was repeated again
with the additional word of "London,"
showing that she hailed from that port.
Passengers paced to and fro under the
awning on the saloon deck, conversing together, or leaning against the rails, pulling at
their cheroots in silence as they scanned the
rapidly changing landscape. The vessel was
the mail steamer bound to London, and
Gerard Clarencourt, Mrs. Devereaux and servants were on board. Quickly she dropped
down stream as the strength of the tide
increased, past Kiddnapore and Diamond
Harbour, between low-lying banks of green
leafy foliage, which far as the eye could
reach were broken by no hills or eminence of
any height, but faded away into distant
stretches of jungle, where the tiger loved still
to lurk. Clusters of low leaf-thatched huts,
shaped like huge bee-hives, half hidden

amidst ferns, banana trees and palms, appeared at intervals. That day passed and
the evening of the next saw the "Simoom"
well on her way. The pilot had left them,
and been rowed on board the brig which
was his floating home, there to await the next
chance which might be met with, by cruising
off the mouth of the river until he should
fall in with another vessel bound for the City
of Palaces. The low outline of Saugor Island
had disappeared astern, and the iron bows of
the steamer, which carried all that Gerard
Clarencourt loved best in the world, cleft the
waters of the Bay of Bengal. The sun was
just lingering upon the edge of the horizon
before disappearing for the night, producing
one of those grand effects of nature which
can scarcely be seen without impressing one
forcibly with a feeling of intense admiration
and wonder. Most of the passengers were on
deck, gazing upon the gorgeous colours arrayed
in one vast and startling panorama before
them. Gerard was leaning over the rail, and a
few feet further off Mrs. Devereaux reclined in

the easiest of cane chairs. Immediately
overhead the sky was of the deepest blue,
gradually toning down as it neared the sun
into the faintest and most delicate tints of sea-
green ; masses of golden clouds were scattered
over this, like tiny fleecy islets and long, narrow streaks of land of brightest gold, in a sea of
exquisite aqua marine. Dark purple clouds
which had assumed the most fantastic and
extravagant forms : here the lofty conical
peaks of a range of mighty mountains reared
their sharp summits, while away to the left
drifted detached masses of vapour, like huge
trees and sailing ships under every stitch of
canvas, and behind these the sun was slowly
disappearing below the edge of the sea, blood
red in hue. And on the glassy, rolling surface
of the ocean was reflected, as in a mirror,
the wondrous hues of the sublimely tinted
heavens.

"*Mon Dieu!* how beautiful! how grandt!"
muttered Julie, Mrs. Devereaux's French
soubrette, from where she stood, down
on the main deck. And Gerard who was

roused by the exclamation, which he heard distinctly, as he happened to be standing immediately above her, turned to address Mrs. Devereaux.

" Fine, isn't it ? " he asked.

"Yes, of course it is ; but to judge from the amount of attention you bestow upon it, one would think that really you had never seen the sun set before. It is too absurd." She went through the little farce of biting her lip, and pouted so prettily at the same time that Gerard, who took the words as a compliment, moved nearer to her.

" Yes ; come and talk to me."

" If you will let me."

" Nonsense ; don't talk rubbish, or you had better go back to your former delightful occupation of craning your neck and peering at the sun. If I didn't want you I should not ask you."

" You are cross to-night."

" And you are polite. Though, what if I am ? Did I not warn you of my sad eccentricities, and yet you chose to come."

"And would do the same again," he answered, as he leaned over the back of her seat.

"But let me tell you your troubles haven't begun yet; I shall tease you frightfully before we say good-bye in London." The remark smote upon Gerard's ear just as she had intended that it should. The idea of ever leaving her had not occurred to him of late. So happy had he been made by the thought of a life, every hour of which would be spent in the same atmosphere which she breathed, a life in which he should be thrown into constant and close intimacy with her, that he never troubled himself by anticipating evil, or spoiling his bliss by thinking of what ills the future might have in store for him. It was enough that they were together, his cup was brimful to overflowing, but why should she dash over some of the contents by suggesting that they must part? That was what pained him, and that she should do it so heedlessly piqued his vanity. He did not understand—how should he?—the *rôle* that she had allotted to herself.

"By the way, when *you* get there, where
do you intend to go? What shall you do
with yourself? Kill time by a butterfly existence, a round of the theatres, whist at the
clubs, varied by light and dainty little dinners
at the 'Star and Garter,' and a romantic
drive home in the moonlight, with a pretty
woman clutching your arm in nervous dread
of your upsetting her. A pair of bright eyes
gazing into yours, looking all sorts of things
and begging you to be careful for her sake?"

"Is my torture already commencing?" he
asked, as he edged in the words during a
slight pause in her rantipole tirade.

"It is for you to judge of that. But would
you fetch me a shawl? The air is quite chilly,
it makes me shiver. Oh, how I do detest
cold!"

"And yet you are returning to the most
changeable and trying climate in the world."

"I know it."

"But you thought fit to go."

"My health would have given way com-
pletely had I lived longer in Calcutta. Poor

old Maltby—you know Maltby, you met him at my house. How fond he was of me, dear deluded man!" Gerard winced. "Well, the very last time he attended me he told me for a positive fact that nothing but change of air could save me from a decline."

"Do you really mean it? Did he think you so ill?"

Gerard's face as he put the question wore an expression of the deepest concern.

"He did, I can assure you, Mr. Clarencourt." Mrs. Devereaux's face beamed with truth and candour as she told her pretty white lie. Gerard was thinking just then of what he would give to hear her lips utter the two syllables which formed his Christian name, for the formal application of Mr., as he bent over her, sounded strangely harsh. Would he ever be all in all to this woman, he wondered.

"Then you must take the greatest care of yourself," at length he answered.

"And despise shawls or wraps when the air is cold?"

"Forgive me; how thoughtless!"

"Not in the least. Go and get it, and then come back and tell me something about your home in Devonshire."

There was a ring of satire in her voice as she spoke. But he never noticed it as, intent upon his errand, he sprang down the companion, in his haste stumbling over and nearly knocking down two people who were standing together at the foot. One was the French soubrette, the other Wilson, Gerard's servant.

"His home, *his home*. I must induce him to talk of it. It will be a place worth owning, if all that Carelesse said was true, and I don't see any good reason for doubting him. No; Geoffrey's worst fault was that of being a fool. He was too simple, but it was fortunate for me, extremely fortunate. I feel more comfortable now that a few miles of blue water lie between us."

Mrs. Devereaux soliloquized thus to herself while she waited Gerard's return.

"What an age he is! I suppose he can't find it. I know I left it in the cabin. How stupid! I ought to have sent him to find Julie."

"Sorry to have kept you waiting, Mrs. Devereaux, but —— "

"Oh, never mind, I had only just begun to despair of your return, but what delayed you? Have you been flirting with the stewardess? or —— "

"I could not find the wrap in the cabin where you thought you had left it. You tease me most unmercifully. How can you think me guilty of such frivolity?"

"I suppose you are much the same as other men, inconstant ever; the charm of a pretty face being at all times too much for you to resist."

"I hope to prove to you that I am worthy of more lenient judgment," he answered, as he bent over her and threw the wrap about her shoulders.

"Quite impossible that you should ever impress me so favourably. What are you but a man, and as such you must be a flirt. Why, even now, I have not the least doubt

that fair creatures in suburban villas and
daughters of county magnates are bemoaning
your absence, stupid enough to believe that
in you they have at length discovered their
Leander, who shall be capable of swimming
through this world of temptation, and
remain staunch and true to them to the
end. Come now, confide in me. Am I not
right?"

"No, as wholly wrong as it is possible for
you to be."

"I can't believe it. Experience robs one
of romance."

"I told you once that I know of none
who would trouble themselves about my fate
if I never returned to England. The men
who would come and stay with me, and drink
my wine for the simple reason that they
know it to be old and of rare vintage; and
avail themselves of my hospitality because I
happen to have some coverts worth shooting
over; *might* find it in their hearts to discuss
my continued absence or my untimely
decease, as the case might be, but it would

be because they missed the shooting, and not me."

"How terribly cynical you are to night! Yet you shall not wander from the point. Now, tell me; will none of your Devonshire friends (I mean the women of course) be thinking tenderly of you, their hearts pierced by a hidden wound which can only be healed by your re-appearance?"

"If they have been stricken then it is unknown to me," he answered with a laugh. Yet even as he spoke the dainty form and brown eyes of Lilian Fabyn rose up before him, as if to upbraid him for his words, and (could he but have known it) she was thinking of him then, and praying in her inmost heart that he might be brought back to her, and sighing for the time, which she fondly hoped would come some day, when he should return her love. What a kindly mercy it is that we frail human beings, so entirely dependent upon the surroundings in which we are placed, the good or ill which may betide us, should

be debarred from knowing what the future
has in store, and that a great and fathomless
gulf should intervene, presenting an impass-
able barrier to prevent us from crossing and
exploring that shadowy land of doubt which
lies beyond the present. Had Lilian Fabyn
possessed the power of gazing into futurity,
of looking ahead a few short weeks only,
her life would have been a load well-nigh
too heavy to bear. And all but that life
she would have gladly given to have been
able to pull down to the ground with her
trembling fingers the barrier, daily increasing
in strength and solidity, which was steadily
rearing its head, to separate from her the
hopes she fondly cherished. She would have
sickened and turned away from reading *what
more* the shifting sands of time could have in
store for her.

Gerard's thoughts had wandered for a brief
space away to the breezy uplands of Devon,
to the deep, shady hollows and lanes where
stood Clifford's Wood, the home that he loved
so well. And imagination drew for him the

cold, proud face of his mother as he had seen her last. But the sound of Mrs. Devereaux's voice recalled him to himself.

" How dull and preoccupied you seem to-night."

" Do you think so ? "

" Yes."

" Then I *must* be horribly boorish, but you will pardon me."

" No, I won't. Why should I ? You do not deserve forgiveness. You have smoked half a cheroot at least, and have never troubled yourself to address one civil remark to me."

" Be merciful, even as you hope for mercy," he laughed.

" I shall die of *ennui* before the voyage is ended. Why, the first week has not passed, and I am beginning to feel *triste* and bored. I shall have to get up a flirtation with that withered-looking Civil Service man, to kill time."

Gerard glanced over his shoulder, but could nowhere see the shrivelled individual alluded to by Mrs. Devereaux, so returned to the charge.

"You are not going below so soon, are you?"

"Yes; this night air chills me through, and is insupportable with such a dull companion."

"Give me one more chance. Stay ten minutes longer, and I will do my utmost to make myself agreeable," pleaded Gerard, as a sudden idea struck him.

"It would be useless."

"Try me."

"To-morrow, Mr. Clarencourt, you shall be put to the test, and I have no doubt you will come off with flying colours."

Gerard offered his escort down the companion ladder, and a thrill of pleasure shot through his veins as she accepted it, and her soft white arm rested on his. At the entrance to her cabin, she gave him her hand and said:

"Good-night, Mr. Clarencourt; that you can be as pleasant as one could wish I know, so do your best when we meet on deck in the morning. It will never do for you and me to play at cross purposes."

He longed to fold her in his arms there and then, to pour into her ears the oft-told story, and learn from her lips that his confessions of love were not in vain. Another moment, and she was gone. The thin partition which shut her off from him had closed, and Gerard retraced his steps along the narrow passage which led to her berth, and returned to the deck.

"Had she only stayed," he muttered, "I would have told her how I love her. I must know; this suspense is harder to bear than the knowledge of the worst. She *shall* be my wife," he added, as he lit another cigar and commenced a solitary walk up and down the deck. Never in all his life had he felt such uncertainty; never had he been so undecided or experienced such want of confidence in himself. It was not like him; by nature he was resolute. He could have expressed his determination on any subject on which he had duly reflected, without the slightest hesitation, relying on his own perspicacity and sound judgment. Here he was at fault. He could not summon courage to tell this woman that he loved her, though he had made up his mind (or thought he had) a score of times. Whenever the opportunity came, he had always let it slip by, too nervous to trust himself; afraid of the plunge he was taking, or the chilling answer he might receive. To confess one's love for a woman ; to ask her to take with you the most important and irretrievable step in life ; to make the leap, the depth of which it is impossible to gauge, must, or ought to be, a stride—the length and cost of which has been well counted ; and the man who might with steady hand and with his feet thrust home in the stirrups rush his horse at the biggest bullfinch with the coolest precision, or stand for hours exposed to a galling fire from the enemy without moving a muscle to indicate anything like fear, may well pause and swerve, and finally beat an ignominious retreat when focussed by a pair of bright eyes and hedged up

in a corner, by the idea which spite of him
will assert itself: that it is just on the cards
that his sentiments are not reciprocated, and
that consequently he may have to retire looking ·uncommonly sheepish and woefully crest-
fallen.   Or what if the fair lady before whose
shrine he is about to bow has only been keeping her hand in, and exercising her well-known
flirting propensities, as she has done already
upon Slingsby, of the Blues, little Tom Chafton,
who really was horribly smitten, and a score
of others?   Or worse still, in thinking he will
try to win a being who will prove to him a
boon and a blessing, a lover and a friend in
one, it is just possible that the dear girl
whose character he has endeavoured to make
a study of (though at the end of his close
scrutiny he is forced to admit to himself he is
little wiser than on the day they met), may
be sailing under false colours.   And he to his
woe may find (but, alas! too late) that while
fishing for a luxury, for which he was about
to exchange his pleasant bachelor quarters,
he has caught a tartar that will test his adroit-

ness to the utmost limits to shake off again.
No doubt, when in the heat of the *mêlée*,
many lose their heads and jump with their
eyes shut and their hearts in their mouths, and
thus the matrimonial list is swelled. All these
and every other kind of doubt entered
Gerard's mind, as with quick stride, and while
accommodating himself to the roll of the ship,
he continued his solitary walk. He tried to
recall the words she had used, the looks she
had given him; all that might bid him hope.
But against these appeared a formidable array
of her sayings and doings which drove him to
distraction, and sent him to his couch, long
after eight bells had rung out upon the night,
perturbed and restless, and though little inclined to sleep, resolute upon one point, that
he would learn his fate ere the sun of the morrow set. But more was to happen in those
few hours than he ever dreamed of. While
the sound of Gerard's footsteps echoed above
her head, Mrs. Devereaux was holding a conversation with Julie, her maid, which evidently
possessed interest for her. She had, she

thought, in the person of the soubrette a faithful ally and *confidante*, whom she could trust implicitly, and to her she had in plain language hinted that it would materially benefit her interests if she could discover, through the agency of Wilson, any facts which would throw a light upon Gerard Clarencourt's position and antecedents, in short, anything and everything which she could learn of his past history. Julie was an apt pupil, and willing enough to enter into the spirit of the thing, not only from a liking which she secretly felt for her mistress, but because she saw an opening for an adventure on her own account. She was pretty, dark haired, with eyes black as sloes, and with all the sparkling, vivacious temperament so entirely characteristic of her nation. Mrs. Devereaux had, when she spoke to her on the subject, laughingly remarked, that her good looks could not fail to tell upon Wilson's susceptibility. And thus she had contrived to put Julie, who was vain of her appearance and influence over the opposite sex, fairly upon her mettle. One besetting sin the soubrette had, and that was, that she spoke the truth only when it suited her. She had already tried the effect of her blandishments, and failed, but was she going to admit it? Not likely! She would be wanting in proper pride. She had sought with the aid of her brightest smile, and her most bewitching air, coupled with a lavish display of her rows of white teeth (which she had hitherto found had done immense execution), to sound Wilson, but he had withstood all her arts, and she had been forced to leave him, none the wiser for her pains. But Julie was ingenious, and did not despair. She was armed with a quick tongue, and rather than own to defeat, was prepared to answer any questions as she thought proper.

"Have you anything to tell me?" asked Mrs. Devereaux the last thing before closing her eyes, addressing the soubrette.

"What would madame wish to know?"

"About Mr. Clarencourt. Have you heard anything about him?"

"But yes, madame."

" What ? "

" Monsieur Wilson, he tell me every-thing."

" I am sleepy ; tired of that horrid saloon deck, the stupid people, and the incessant din of the engines. Answer my question straightforwardly."

But Mademoiselle Julie was by no means prepared to end the conversation so abruptly. She intended to have *her* gossip before she retired to rest. She was not tired of her life on the steamer. The steward paid her much attention, not to speak of others ; be-sides she was determined to bring Wilson under subjection.

" Must I tell madame all at once ? " she asked cunningly.

" Yes, of course, you stupid girl ; who else does it concern but me ? Repeat to me what Wilson said." Julie thought a moment and then spoke.

" Well, madame, Wilson tell me that Monsieur Clarencourt is very rich."

" Yes."

"He have thousands and thousands."

"Well?"

"He have large park, what madame call estate."

Julie was simply repeating what her sharp ears had picked up of a conversation between her· mistress and Geoffrey Carelesse, part of which she had heard by eavesdropping.

Mrs. Devereaux was annoyed. Of course, it was not new to her.

"Is that all you have learned? because it amounts to nothing."

"But no, madame. Wilson tell me all about large, grandt place in Ireland, and that the family of Clarencourt is ancient and honourable."

"That will do, Julie. Good-night; you may save yourself the trouble of telling me more of what I already know. Make better use of your time in future. I shall know how to reward you, so don't forget."

Mrs. Devereaux rested her fair head upon her pillow and fell to thinking. Think-

ing of what she would do with those vast
estates when she became mistress of them,
and she never for a moment doubted
that she should occupy that position. Could
it be otherwise? did he not love her? She
was sure of that. She had but to wait
patiently, and all that he had would be
hers. She never bestowed a thought on
the pain and the anguish it would cause
him if he ever learned that she did
not love him. What did it matter to
her if she wrecked his life by winning
his heart, only to fling it from her when
it suited her convenience? Once the money
in her hands (at least to some extent) she
would let him understand that maudlin
sentiment was not in her line. They would
get on very well together. She would take
care of that, because it would be essential
to her plans to keep in with him, or who
would supply the money for her town house,
her villa in the South, box at the opera,
servants, carriages, and a thousand other
little odds and ends, all of which she had

set her heart upon. But love-making or affection after they were married was not to be thought of. One thing piqued Mrs. Devereaux, for like many people who are beautiful she was proud and vain of her appearance to an absurd degree, and that any man for whom she had chosen to show a decided preference should have resisted her charms, without flinging himself at her feet and acknowledging his weakness, annoyed her and wounded her *amour propre*. She cared nothing for him, had a heart above such absurdities, but he should cringe to her yet, and with this thought she fell asleep.

CHAPTER X.

In cloudless splendour the morning broke. The wind had freshened and hauled aft, and Davis, the captain, had ordered sail to be made, and with a spanking breeze on the quarter, the "Simoom" bounded along on the starboard tack under steam and sail, her course shaped for Old England, her snowy clouds of canvas bellying, and dashing fountains of spray into the air as she clove her way through the mighty masses of surging water. Far astern a track of seething, bubbling foam, and eddying, miniature whirlpools marked her track, and screaming sea birds hovered in her wake, swooping down with piercing cries to glut their ravenous appetites with dainty morsels stirred up and brought to the surface by the iron monster's keel. The skipper paced the bridge and conned the ship. Busy life on board the great mail boat had begun, and seamen hurried along the decks, or swarmed like bees in the weather rigging, rattling down, with hitch and seizing. Shoals of flying fish rose from the dancing waters, and scudded away to leeward, chased by their mortal and relentless foes, the albacore and dolphin. Groups of passengers were gathered in knots, discussing trivial subjects, the last piece of scandal, or the latest news they had gleaned before leaving Calcutta and forgotten to relate. Peals of laughter rang out from several men who had collected in the smoke-room, and who were listening to witty jests and racy stories told by one of their number. Others were lounging on easy cane settees, too lazy or listless to do aught else, or possibly preferring their own thoughts to trying to force a conversation when nothing remained to be told. Gerard Clarencourt had sauntered on deck as usual, but to his annoyance found that Mrs. Devereaux had carried out her

threat of flirting, or amusing herself, and was
doing so at the expense of a circle of
men she had collected about her. What
pretty widow could be on board a steamer,
boasting a fair complement of the male sex,
without attracting due attention and admiration from so varied an assortment of in-
flammable material? There were army men
returning for a few months' leave, yellow-
skinned, "jaundiced" looking tea planters
from up country, Civil Service men, wealthy
merchants, who had made their pile and
were going back to the old country for rest,
perhaps to look out for a wife to superin-
tend the neat little villa on the Thames which
they meant to buy, and help them slacken
their purse-strings in search of a fashionable
existence. Besides, Mrs. Devereaux was more
than pretty ; she was a beauty, though
of a haughty and proud type. She walked
and talked as though she were cognizant
of that important fact, and intended to
exact due homage. No stranger could
pass her by without a second glance and

a desire to know more about her—who
she was—and experience a longing to look
again upon her clear-cut patrician features.
So Mrs. Devereaux had been well discussed
and everybody knew everything that was to be
learned about her before the Saugor light had
sunk astern and the ship was well clear of the
river.   Considerable jealousy had been generally felt amongst the males that Gerard should
have monopolized so much of the fair widow's
attention, and so not one of her devotees felt
inclined to budge an inch when they saw him
appear.   Gerard took in the whole situation
at a glance, and seeing that there was not
the least chance of a *tête-à-tête*, walked up
and down once or twice, and then, thinking
that a quiet cheroot in the smoke-room would
be the best thing under the circumstances,
found that he had left his cigar case in his
berth.   He dived down to fetch it, intending
to carry out his programme, when the sound
of Wilson's voice attracted his attention.   As
he drew near to his own door, which was
hooked back to prevent it from slamming, he

paused to listen for a moment, rather amused, as Wilson was evidently talking to himself.

"The impertinent hussy, the brazen-faced minx, to think that I should let on to *her* about Mr. Gerard.   But I can't say nothin'; my hands are tied.   Didn't I tell him as how I would never take it upon myself to interfere again when he took on so wild last time? Didn't I tell him that, and didn't he sort o' forgive me?   And here, he's as blind as a bat, and as mad as any March hare after that woman, and me not able to warn nor set him up to her tomfooleries.   It's a nice state o' things to put her maid on to findin' out about one's master."   Gerard had heard quite enough to make him impatient, so he entered his berth.

"Get me my cigar case, Wilson ; I think I must have left it in the pocket of that coat hanging up."

"Yes, sir."

"And, Wilson."

"Here it is, sir," said the man as he handed Gerard the missing article.

13—2

"Is there anything else that I can get you, Mr. Gerard? 'cause I was going to make bold to go up on deck, if so be as you didn't want me. I've tidied the berth, sir, and laid away all the things nice and straight."

"No, I don't want anything else." Gerard was irresolute for an instant; should he question the man or not?

"Thank ye, sir."

"But, Wilson, stay one moment, I have something to say to you."

"Yes, Mr. Gerard."

"What were you saying to yourself just as I entered?"

"It's only a bad habit as I've got into of late, but I don't rightly remember what it was all about, some nonsense o' my own, like enough."

"Think again. I have reasons to believe that it concerns me."

"I'd rather hold my tongue, sir; pity I can't when I'm alone, no good can come o' me speakin'."

"No harm can when I wish you to do so, and the subject refers to me."

"Well, sir, it was just all along of that Julie. Now I said as I would never no more interfere nor say nothin', but it's your wish, sir, so it's right for certain this time."

"Go on."

"Well, Julie, that's Mrs. Devereaux's maid, came a-bummin' about me, a-wantin' to be friendly; well, I didn't like to be stand off; she seemed a nice young woman, at first like, but she don't improve upon acquaintance, for the day afore yesterday, and yesterday and this mornin', she've been saucy fit to rile a fellow, sir."

"What has she done?"

"Just asked me all manner o' questions about you, Mr. Gerard."

"About me?"

"Yes, sir."

"What were they?"

"Whether you was rich."

"Yes."

"And how much land you had, and the

sort o' style you lived in down at Clifford's Wood and over in Ireland."

"And what answer did you make her?"

"Just told her nothin' but what I was proud to tell, and what wouldn't hurt you, Mr. Gerard; that you come o' a good old family as dates back many a year, and one as has served its country afore now at a pinch."

"Well, I don't see any harm in that; Julie likes a gossip, that's all."

"You can't go for to think that Julie is at the bottom o' it. My blood just biled. She never thought o' askin' so much without bein' put up to it. There ain't no millstone to look through, Mr. Gerard, it's all right plain before you, you can't miss seein' of it. It's Mrs. Devereaux's doin', for certain."

"Wilson, you will remember what I said to you on a former occasion." The dangerous steel-grey light flashed in Gerard's eyes as he spoke. "You will recollect that then I told you never to mention such absurdities to me again. The ideas which you hint at are simply preposterous. Let me hear no more of them. I absolve you from all blame, because it was my wish that you should speak; but take care that you keep your ridiculous surmises to yourself for the future."

" Very well, Mr. Gerard."

" See that you don't forget what I have said."

" As you wish, sir; I've done all I can to save you from ruinin' yourself with your eyes shut—for your father's sake, sir, the years as I served him, and for yours. And, as sure as you stands where you are, you'll rue the day as you met Mrs. Devereaux."

" Thanks for your anxiety, Wilson; I know you mean it well, but there is no earthly necessity for you to distress yourself on my account. Perhaps your words may prove prophetic; I don't think they will, but say no more on the subject, and keep your own counsel as to my affairs." Gerard shrugged his shoulders incredulously as he spoke, as if the bare idea of harm happening to him through Mrs. Devereaux was highly ludicrous.

Wilson left the berth with a sorrowful expression on his honest face, as if he were quite convinced that now nothing could intervene to save his master, or stop his downward course to perdition. He had been very miserable of late. The gladness that he felt at the prospect of once again seeing the old walls of Clifford's Wood, which he loved as well as if they belonged to him, was marred by the anxiety he experienced on Gerard's account. He had watched Mrs. Devereaux narrowly since they had left Calcutta, and he had had every facility for observing her most trifling gesture. He was near when none thought of him, and he prowled and hung around, feeling agitated and miserable. It might have been instinct which led him to dread Mrs. Devereaux's influence over Gerard, but that it was growing he had no doubt. He knew how passionate, impulsive and kindly his master was by nature, and he feared with inward terror that *she* should awaken love in his heart, that *she* should call all his hot, headstrong emotions into life. Where would it end? What would become of him when his eyes were opened, and he read the terrible truth and suffered the bitter anguish of spirit that would come upon him when he knew that she had never loved him, and that he was indissolubly chained to a woman who cared only for his gold? It is not necessary for a person to be highly cultured to be able to form a very fair estimation of character in its broadest points. Wilson knew nothing of grammar, but he recognized the outward semblance of truth and honesty when he saw it; the country yokel can do the same. And that Mrs. Devereaux lacked those qualities he would have staked his life. He had seen the two together often latterly. Gerard, as he hung over her chair, and drank in her words, and listened to her most trivial remarks, *loved* her, that was plainly evident; but the other, with her soft, winning smile and parted lips, as she looked in *his* face, was different when she thought none saw her; then Wilson had seen a cold, pitiless look cross her features, like the shadow thrown by a cloud over a beautiful

landscape, which robbed it of its bright effects
and brilliant colours, and left it barren, wild,
and uninteresting.

The one he recognized as genuine, the
other as false. He had seen enough of the
world to discriminate, and that Mrs. Devereaux
did not love in return he was sure. But
Wilson saw no way to stop the course of
events, so went about his work with sighs
and a sad foreboding of ill. Gerard, once
alone, fell to thinking for a few minutes as
if what he had heard had made some slight
impression, but if it had, it was but momentary.
It was not in his nature to harbour doubts
where he gave his love. That *she* could be
base or sordid, that *she* could be mean
enough to hanker after his wealth, he could
not and would not believe. Such thoughts
were cowardly and unworthy in him. He
smiled at them as he thought. He loved
blindly, dazzled by the beauty of her face,
by the witchery of her smiles. Her form
rose up before him in shadowy outline,
voluptuous and fair, and his soul burned

within him to possess her. He would seek
her and learn his fate. With this idea
Gerard sought the deck. Fortune favoured
him at the moment, or seemed to, for Mrs.
Devereaux, who probably thought that she
might carry the game too far and pique
Gerard's feelings rather more than would
suit her plans, had contrived to dismiss her
numerous admirers on various ingenious
pretexts and was alone. She looked more
lovely than ever, he thought, as she reclined
gracefully in her wicker chair. The soft
folds of some white clinging material, just
relieved from sameness by ribbons of
pale blue, revealed to advantage the exquisite moulding of her bust and shoulders.
And Gerard's heart beat quickly as he
moved towards her.

"Where have you been playing truant?"
she asked with a laugh.

"From whom?"

"Me! of course."

"I came on deck, but you were too
much occupied to notice me."

"With those stupid men, I suppose you mean."

"Yes."

"Well, I had to be civil to them."

"And leave me to curse my luck and them in the same breath."

"I hope you did nothing so wicked."

"I could have flung them overboard one after the other, deaf to their appeals for mercy. I felt so horribly put out when I saw the idiots swarming about you."

"Flies will seek the honey, you know, and, poor fellows, they can't help themselves."

"Oh! I don't blame them."

"How could you with justice?"

"Well, they must look out for the spiders! I felt awfully like punching their heads all round, but instead——"

"Ah, what did you do instead? Give an account of yourself."

"Growled and smoked in my own berth."

"And left me to the tender mercies of others. Is that fulfilling the promise you made to me in Calcutta? You were to be at my beck and call, fetch me my fan or anything that I wanted, read to me, and stay with me the whole day."

"Do you want me to do so?" asked Gerard in a subdued key.

"If I didn't, would you be here now? Should I have asked you to come? How can you ask?"

This was a clear case of throwing down the gauntlet, and no mistake, and she accompanied her words with a seductive glance and a trick she had of veiling her turquoise-blue eyes with a languid droop of the long, fringed lids, that few men could have withstood, and, least of all, one so inexperienced and susceptible as Gerard. You could not blame the lad. There was scarce a man on board who could have resisted such beauty as she possessed, had she chosen to add him to the list of her conquests. Scarce one of them, including captain and passengers, who could have looked on those waving masses of fair hair, and scented the delicate perfume she always used, and seen the soft, pink blush that mantled in her cheeks, like the delicate bloom on the side of a peach, and *felt* the love-light that she could call to her aid, without being vanquished, intoxicated, willing to risk life, honour, and soul, if need be, for *her*. Proud they would have been to think that she had chosen to cast her eyes upon them. Had she taken the motto of Ouida's "Strathmore," "Slay and spare not," few who crossed her path would have done so without good cause to remember her. Then what wonder that Gerard succumbed, that his pulse beat like lightning, his heart like the dull thud of a hammer; while his mouth grew parched and his utterance thick with the emotion that came with her words. She must love him, there could be no doubt now, or why should she speak as she had done? But then the full glare of day was upon them; men were sitting not ten yards away; eyes were on him; he must be guarded, and not let them see what he felt. The thought steadied and nerved him. He had longed for this moment, and it had come at last. His voice had no tremor in it now. The rich blood mounted to his sun-tanned cheeks, and he bent his head low; but save that he was calm, and none could tell—none could know the mad whirl of thoughts that coursed through his brain in wildest confusion as he said:

"You will not think me presumptuous— you cannot blame me for speaking to you. I can bear it no longer. If you care to have me with you, you cannot be quite indifferent to me. Tell me—for God's sake, let me know my fate! Mrs. Devereaux, Ada, I——"

There was a heavy footfall on the deck, and a man's voice rang in Gerard's ears.

"Guess I've found the book, Mrs. Devereaux, that I told you of, though I've had a tall hunt for it. But I was nuts on finding it, and so I just got up some of my bullock trunks, and sure enough it was stowed away right at the bottom. I guess you'll sit like a blue chicken on a pine log, and never move till you've read it right away. I did."

Gerard looked up, and encountered the stare

of two grey eyes, and those same eyes were
deep-set in the head of a broad-shouldered,
jolly-looking American—one of the very
men who had been riling Gerard by buzzing
about Mrs. Devereaux in the earlier part of
the morning. Gerard looked, and as he did
so inwardly he cursed that man, with as
heavy a curse as the Cardinal laid upon the
poor Jackdaw of Rheims. Could that look
have made him as bald as a coote for life,
Gerard would have been pleased at that same
moment. What a fool he felt—what an ass
he looked! No man (short of Job himself)
could have stood an interruption at such a
moment. It must be his luckless destiny—
his *Kismet*—which thus pursued him, and
came between the object of his love. So
thought Gerard as he eyed the Yankee as
though, time and place permitting, he would
have slain him. The worst of it was he
seemed in no hurry to go, for after handing
the book to Mrs. Devereaux, he drew a camp-
stool, which stood unoccupied, near him, and
sat down. Mrs. Devereaux alone seemed

equal to the occasion, though inwardly
she was convulsed with rage that the luckless American, who believed that he was
ingratiating himself in her favour, should
thus have blundered in, and spoilt all by
his untimely appearance, just when the wish
of her heart was about to be realized. It
was enough to make a saint spiteful. And
she did feel sufficiently malicious to wish him
at the bottom of the sea rather than where he
was. But she contrived to control herself,
to answer him civilly, and thank him for his
kindness. After two or three commonplace
remarks, Gerard rose, beside himself with
rage, and walked off to the for'ard rail of the
saloon deck. He noticed that one of the
men had crawled out along the foot-rope of
the fore upper topsail yard, and was astride
of the port yard-arm. He turned away, about
to quit the deck, put out with every one, but
the Yankee in particular, upon whose devoted
head he still continued to pour anathemas,
when he heard a shriek, wild and piercing in
its cadence. He glanced round, and instinc-

tively looked at the upper topsail yard, where an instant before the sailor had sat. A horrible sight met his gaze. The man had lost his hold, and round and round in mid-air his body whirled. He struck the water, and as he rose to the surface Gerard saw that he was but an indifferent swimmer. The poor wretch would sink! No thought of danger to himself ever entered his brain in the quick flash of thought. The man would perish, with none to help, and before his very eyes! It could not be! Should he look on and watch him drown? In another instant Gerard had flung off his coat, and plunged into the sea.

CHAPTER XI.

THE BREAKWOOD FÊTE.

LADY FABYN had not mistaken the meaning of the mental suffering which had convulsed Lilian's face, like a spasm of agony, on that night when she had expressed to her daughter her wish that she should accept the attentions paid to her so openly by the future Lord Goddington, and become his wife. Her worst suspicions had been confirmed. Lilian's heart was not in her own keeping. But who had committed the theft? Who had robbed her of her daughter? Who had dared to venture to tamper with the affections of Miss Lilian Fabyn of The Towers, without the knowledge of Sir George or herself? That was what Lady Fabyn would have very much liked to know. Her character was like many commonly to be met with in every day existence, and was

11—2

chalked out on broad and convenient lines to suit her own comfort. She was purse-proud, proud of the position she occupied in the county, proud of her own ability and tact in having elevated herself somewhat in the social scale—though she was the daughter of a gentleman well-to-do and worthy—by her marriage with Sir George. She was not dictatorial or domineering, provided that people fell in with her views and ways of thinking, and pandered to (what she was pleased to consider) her superior knowledge and keener powers of discrimination. And generally speaking she would have passed for being good-natured, but in reality that estimable quality, only made its appearance when her wishes were attended to, and she was allowed to have her own way. It is too often the case in this world ; people are saints outwardly if you only *agree* with them, and don't attempt to argue or assert your opinions in any way. But diverge from that beaten track, express contrary views, press home the fact that your *will* must be acknowledged, dispute their all-wise judgment, and what is the effect? They topple from the lofty pinnacle where they had set themselves, their smiles vanish. They try for a rush with the bit in their teeth, and become once again veritable sinners. In this way, what might be a happy home is too often rendered a hot-bed of discontent, misery, and family strife. When two horses harnessed to the same carriage insist upon going in opposite directions what is the result? Confusion, and too probably a smash. And simply because they don't recognize that their ends are the same. They won't pull *together*. Such was not Lady Fabyn's position at The Towers however. Sir George was much too good-tempered and easy-going to dispute or quibble with his wife's foibles. Provided that she did not interfere with his mode of life he was content, but rather than come to high words he would have waived the dispute with cheery good-nature and with a smile on his frank, ruddy face. And so their connubial bliss remained intact. Lady

Fabyn had kept her own counsel and had
not mentioned to Sir George the discovery
she had made. When she had acquiesced in
Lilian's desire to return to Sidcombe without
opposition it was entirely owing to the fact
that she knew the Honourable Jim had
betaken himself to Breakwood. She had
been willing enough that Lilian should
remain in town while he was there. But she
chuckled in her sleeve, and was secretly
delighted at the turn which events took,
when Sir George proposed to go back to
Sidcombe and take Lilian with him. It was
just what Lady Fabyn wanted. She would
have suggested returning herself, but then
she would have had to relinquish her own
pleasures, to sacrifice herself, for what she
deemed to be Lilian's welfare. That was
beyond her. For once her schemes ran
counter to her own personal desires. So to
her delight Sir George got tired of London,
and wished to exchange it for the country
just in the nick of time. Breakwood, Lord
Goddington's place, was only a short distance

from The Towers, in fact, the two estates joined, and the Honourable Jim, as was his wont, would drop in to see Sir George, and so the young people would meet. Failing the hooking of the Honourable Jim, or putting him on one side altogether, Lady Fabyn would have handed Lilian over to the keeping of another man. But it would have been necessary that that more highly-favoured individual should have been of yet more exalted rank, and have possessed moreover a longer purse than Jim Ledsham ever would, before she could have been tempted to throw over the future Lord Goddington of Breakwood and Eton Square. Lady Fabyn was right. He was un-doubtedly a great catch, and she fully intended to lose no chance of landing him if she could help it. With that view she curtailed her visit somewhat and re-joined Sir George. She had scrutinized every action of her daughter's since that memorable night when Lilian had amazed her by the way in which she had flared up and given her a taste of her pluck and spirit, though it had ended, as is general in such cases, in tears. Her letters had all been most systematically brought first to Lady Fabyn before they were delivered to their owner. And even in her walks and rides Lillian had been as much as was possible under surveillance. But with all her shrewdness Lady Fabyn had been forced to admit to herself that her sagacity was at fault. She could discover nothing. And her questions to Lilian had been productive of no more than short answers which left her as wise as she was before. For once in her life Lady Fabyn had to acknowledge herself fairly nonplussed. But she began to take heart, and to hope that her daughter had seen the wisdom of submitting to her will and authority, when one day an invitation to a garden party had come from Breakwood. Telegrams had been received from Cannes to the effect that Lord Goddington was recovering, and so her ladyship would be glad to see them. She handed the note across the table in silence to Lilian, who read it through and quietly expressed her willingness to go. Here was another mystery which fairly puzzled Lady Fabyn. If she did not wish to have anything to do with Mr. Ledsham, if she did not like him, why did she signify her pleasure at the prospect of visiting there? The only construction that could be put upon her behaviour was that Lilian had thought better of it and would carry out her mother's wishes. So thought Lady Fabyn, and she was overjoyed. Never was her acumen, on which she prided herself, more at fault. The day of the Breakwood festivity had arrived and Lilian was alone in the drawing-room at The Towers. It wanted a couple of hours to the time at which they had arranged to start, when Lady Fabyn entered with both her hands full of flowers which she began to arrange in an old china bowl. She wished to speak to her daughter upon the subject uppermost in her mind, but she was rather at a loss how to open the ball.

"Lilian, dear," she said in a cooing voice. Lady Fabyn always cooed when she wanted her own way, and was doubtful whether she would get it without a struggle.

"Yes, mother."

"Isn't it fearfully close and oppressive?"

"I don't feel it."

"No! I think we shall have a storm before long"—perhaps it was due to her own thoughts, that were brewing for a climax—"so much electricity in the atmosphere."

"Do you think so? I hope not," answered Lilian.

"I am sure of it. I can always tell; my head aches invariably. It will be so provoking. Everything will be spoilt. And poor Lady Goddington, I quite pity her; she will be so put out."

"Yes, it would be a pity. But, mother, I don't think the sky looks like rain. It is quite bright and clear over the sea," answered

Lilian, as she got up and went to one of the
windows.

"Nonsense, child. I tell you I am sure of
it." There was no necessity to answer the
last remark, so the girl went on quietly with
her work. Lady Fabyn dexterously placed
some lilies close to a sprig of scarlet geranium,
over which hung sprays of maidenhair fern,
and then, with her head on one side, stepped
back a pace, to admire the effect. The
artistic groupings of her flowers pleased her,
but Lilian's silence did not, so she began again.

"I think the dress you are going to wear,
dear, suits you admirably. The colours are
the very thing with your hair and complexion." Lilian sighed wearily. The subject
had no interest for her. She was going to
the garden party with an object, certainly,
but there would be no one there whom she
cared to please. The whole affair would be
an ordeal for her. Would she not have to
suffer the boredom of attentions from Jim
Ledsham, and that, too, under her mother's
eye, as it were?

"I am glad you think the dress becoming, mother," she answered at length ; but the listless apathy with which she spoke did not escape Lady Fabyn's quick ears. She turned round sharply, and looked at her daughter, but her face was hidden as she bent over her needle.

"Child, what is the matter? Don't you care to go to Lady Goddington's?"

"Of course I do, mother. We have talked of little else for days." Lilian hated herself for the reply the moment after she had made it. But she must dissemble ; she could not be constantly at war with her mother. Of late she had felt out of spirits and thoroughly miserable, and, besides, where was the use of further bickering about Mr. Ledsham? She had expressed her feelings frankly and without reserve—she would have none of him. She had determined upon a more decided course of action when the right moment arrived. Her reply pleased Lady Fabyn. She read in it, she thought, less opposition, and inwardly she resolved to let events

take their course for the present. Lilian
went off to her own room, and appeared
again only when the carriage which was to
convey them to Breakwood drove round to
the door. Little was said during the drive,
though Lady Fabyn seemed in the best of
spirits, and chatted away incessantly, but
Lilian was engrossed with her own thoughts.
As they swung along in the family
barouche, memory reverted to the time, only
a year ago, when she had driven on that same
road, and on identically the same errand, but
with what widely different feelings? Then
she had felt light-hearted, joyous. Yet the
only difference was that then she was
going where she knew she should meet
Gerard Clarencourt; but now he was in
India for all she knew to the contrary,
and she was speeding along those lanes
wholly and solely for the purpose of learning
something of him. The earliest reminiscences
of her childish years teemed with recollections
of Gerard, of games of play, of happy hours
spent together on the Sidcombe beach, where

with bare legs they wandered hand-in-hand midst the deep, cool pools of water on the Shark's Tooth reef, bent on the capture of shrimps and tiny fish with which to stock a miniature aquarium, or dug and romped for hours on the golden sands, without a care, without a thought, save that of bliss. What bursts of infant laughter had those tall cliffs re-echoed, grim witnesses of all those gladsome hours, now gone for ever? But the intimacy which had existed between the two families, or, at all events, between the younger members of them in those earlier years, when no harm, as Lady Fabyn thought, could come of it, was a thing of the past of late. Gerard might have been a good enough match for her daughter under some circumstances, but there was a bigger fish in the water, and so Lady Fabyn judged it wise to take such judicious steps, by degrees, as would lead to a gradual breaking-off of the old terms of friendship, which had lasted long enough, for prudence sake. Mrs. Clarencourt, although she did not trouble herself much about her child, or who he played with, so long as it was with children of his own station in life, was not slow to take offence, and so the coldness of a chill reserve and distantly polite formality had arisen, and this very fact accounted for Lilian's sole purpose in going to Breakwood. She wished to gain information concerning the movements of her old playmate, who had gradually and almost unknown to her crept into her heart and occupied the first place there. Owing to the existing state of affairs Lilian, much as she would have liked, could not call at Clifford's Wood alone, and she feared to betray her real feelings before her mother. She knew that Mrs. Clarencourt had returned. In a small gossiping town like Sidcombe, such an event as the arrival from London of the mistress of Clifford's Wood spread like wildfire. That she should most probably meet her at Breakwood she felt confident, because Mrs. Clarencourt was on close terms of intimacy with her ladyship, and would hardly be absent from such a gay and important gathering, unless she were ill. Lilian would see her, and in a commonplace way inquire after her son, and thus hear some authentic account of his doings. Should she ever be so light-hearted again, she wondered—should she ever know what it was to be so entirely free from care as in those youthful days? Poor child! she was little more in years, now barely eighteen. Yet, had she known it, she had quitted *for ever* those pleasant paths. She had trodden for the last time in those footmarks where she had been exempt from pain, where no gnawing anguish had preyed upon her, and had boldly launched out into the sea of life, set her sails and shaped her course for a point where the wind and tide would admit of *no return*. And that change had taken place when, unknown to her, she had bestowed her heart upon Gerard beyond recall. She was capable of erecting an idol for herself, of putting forth her strength and clinging with all the power of her nature, with all the depth of feeling which belonged to her, to the hero she had created *but once.* She loved blindly, with no apparent hope; but it was beyond her control now to pluck from her heart the image she had placed there. She had made her choice and, come weal or woe, she could make no other. Her nature had received a shock (the effects of which nothing had as yet obliterated) that night when her mother had so clumsily shown her hand and shone forth in her true colours. It was not so much the words used by Lady Fabyn that had pained Lilian; she had contrived to bridle her temper, but she had not been sufficiently mistress of herself to mask her face, and Lilian would have been slow indeed had she failed to read what was written upon it. From that moment she felt that she need look for little sympathy from that quarter. Lady Fabyn had never taken the trouble to try to understand or sift her daughter's nature. She had been a good mother, as mothers go. The child had always possessed everything that she could desire to make her happy, and she had been denied no pleasures. But to supply them had given Lady Fabyn no trouble. It is easy to surround one's family with every luxury from the contents of a well-filled purse; but is it possible for people to be such fools as to think that in that way alone they can gain the affections and the confidence of their children? Are they to be bought? Surely not. Yet there are many such parents. And that fact most probably supplies the reason why filial affection of the present day is so scarce and so little to be depended upon. Society takes up so much of their time. Dear Lady C. or Lord B. demands their attention, and they have little left to bestow upon their children. This had been precisely the case with Lilian; every comfort that money could buy had been lavished upon her, but Lady Fabyn's life and conduct had been such as to cause very few feelings of confidence or trust to emanate from the daily intercourse. She had done nothing to strengthen the home ties or to bind her child to her by awakening in her heart sentiments of love and *friendship*. If she had, no secrets would ever have sprung up between her and Lilian. She meant no harm, doubtless; she was selfish, that was all. And so but little had been necessary to widen the gap and estrange them. Lilian sat silent in her corner of the carriage, paying no more attention than the bare dictates of courtesy required to the vapid gossipings indulged in by her mother. The nearest lodge-gate by which they could approach the house was at some distance from The Towers, for Lord Goddington possessed many a broad acre of rich pasturage, dotted with noble oaks of giant girth and of fabulous age, where the cattle browsed knee deep in the long, sweet grass and fragrant clover; many a rood of shady forest and bracken-covered hillside, where the red deer roamed at will, free as on its native slopes of Exmoor; many a covert and outlying plantation, where a fine old dog fox

could generally be found, tough of limb and
sound enough of wind to try the mettle and
staying powers of the best hunters that ever
were foaled, if they were to keep the pack
in sight and be well in at the death. At
length they quitted the road and drove
through a massive stone-pillared entrance,
the iron gates of which were flung open by a
ruddy-faced, cleanly-clad woman, and behind
her, in the porch of the cottage, stood a
cluster of flaxen-haired, rosy-cheeked children, who peeped out shyly and curtseyed
deferentially as the great people passed by.
Lilian would have liked to stop the carriage
and address a few words of kindness, but
she was forced to content herself, since Lady
Fabyn was present, with a good-natured
nod and a pleasant smile as they swept
past, and entered a double avenue of wide-
spreading birch and elms which flanked the
broad, well-kept gravel drive that led up
to the front entrance of Breakwood. They
were by no means amongst the first of the
arrivals, for already the smoothly shaven

lawns were dotted with fashionably attired
ladies. A bright-coloured marquee stood
invitingly placed under a clump of trees for
the accommodation of those who might wish
to regale themselves with ices, creams,
jellies, claret, champagne cup, and scores
of other good things which it is needless to
mention; for Lady Goddington, when she
did a thing, did it well. Coloured rugs
and soft cushions were laid about on the
turf, for such as chose to lounge or flirt
instead of indulging in tennis or the much-
despised croquet which was going for the
older people. The gardens were brilliant
with bright-hued flowers, and shady alleys
led off to a delightful maze of woodland, in
which those who cared to lose themselves
might do so to perfection and without fear
of interruption. Where the graceful, undu-
lating slopes of the lawn merged into the
park, the waters of a lake, fringed with
variegated foliage, sparkled in the sunlight;
stately swans and bright plumed birds
sought shelter on the tiny islets, or reposed

sedately in the shade. Boats shaped like Venetian gondolas, with silken awnings, were not wanting to tempt the belles from the shelter of their chaperones' wings. And tesselated paved conservatories, filled with lovely exotics, palms, and ferns, over which trickled bright cascades from fountains half buried in leaves, were to be found by those who cared to seek them, intent on whisperings and a wealth of words which none might listen to. Lady Goddington, a stately peeress of some fifty summers, received her guests as they alighted from every description of vehicle, dressed in a quiet but elegant costume. After addressing the few necessary words to their hostess in reply to her kindly welcome, Lilian and Lady Fabyn mingled with the throng collected on the grass. They were known to most of the people there, and Lady Fabyn was soon busily engaged in conversation with a circle of her most intimate friends. The chance was not to be lost, and Lilian left her mother and went in search of Mrs. Clarencourt whom she soon discovered, and alone. They exchanged the customary words of greeting, and Lilian sat down by her side.

"How insufferably hot it is, dear. Quite oppressive. Mr. Ledsham has gone to get me an ice or something. How well you are looking. Lady Fabyn and Sir George are here, I suppose?"

Mrs. Clarencourt liked Lilian, and to do her justice had never changed towards her in manner when they met; she did not choose to visit the sins of the parents upon the child, and she knew that the girl was not to blame for any unpleasantness that had arisen.

"No, only mother," answered Lilian.

"Indeed. Sir George is well, I hope."

"Yes, thanks."

"I met you last in the Row, I think, weeks ago. You know I have only just returned from town. In fact, I altered my arrangements, and ran down a day or two earlier than I had intended, on purpose to be here this afternoon. Dear Lady Goddington is so kind and nice, and we are such very old friends, you know."

Lilian murmured some suitable reply ; she was in momentary dread that Ledsham would re-appear to interrupt their *tête-à-tête*. But much to her joy Mrs. Clarencourt rattled on again, and supplied her with the very information she sought.

" You will be glad to hear that Gerard is well, I had a note from him the other day. Boys are so bad at letter writing as a rule. But he wrote me quite a wonderful account of his doings in Calcutta and the sort of life he was leading."

" I am so glad to hear that his health is good," replied Lilian, while a faint blush which she could not control mounted to her cheeks. Whether it was the tone of her voice or what, which attracted Mrs. Clarencourt's ear, it is impossible to say. Women so easily read each other. But *something* caused her to look at Lilian, their eyes met, and in that one quick glance Mrs. Clarencourt felt assured that her son had awakened more than mere interest in the bosom of the heiress of The Towers. It was wonderful to see with what tact and cleverness Mrs. Clarencourt could cloak her real feelings, and talk about her son as if she cared and thought of him, when in her heart he occupied a less important place than did her favourite French poodle.

"Yes, I thought you would like to hear of your old playmate. You and he used to be inseparable." She kept her eyes fixed on Lilian's face as she spoke, and saw her colour visibly again.

"Does he intend to return soon?" she faltered. "I am sure you must miss him dreadfully, Mrs. Clarencourt."

"Oh yes, I do, but then I must sacrifice myself, you see, dear, if I wish him to travel and know something of the world. Clifford's Wood is almost unbearable to me without him."

"How good of you to spare him."

"Ah, I look to the future to repay me for the loss of him now. The months will soon slip by, and he will return, looking so big and brown, and with so much to say for himself. And I expect wonders from his brush, he used to be so fond of sketching, as you know. He took with him a perfect menagerie of useful things, and amongst them paints and paper were not forgotten."

At this juncture the Honourable Jim came up with an ice and some champagne cup. If the truth must be told he had been searching for Lilian all over the gardens, instead of dancing attendance upon the widow, which accounted for his long absence. But he could scarcely conceal his annoyance when he found her with Mrs. Clarencourt. He doubted his ability to separate the two women, for he had intended to appropriate Lilian to himself for the afternoon, and here his little plans were frustrated. But he was not to be done.

"Let me get you something, Miss Fabyn," he said, after they had exchanged a few sentences. Yes; Lilian would take an ice. By the by, what an unchangeable predi-

lection ladies always show for ices ! The only
wonder is that they never apparently suffer
from any bad effects, though they eat them
regardless of high temperature. A happy
thought entered Ledsham's head, as he
returned from the marquee with the coveted
luxury, and he proceeded to put it into
effect.

"I want you to come and admire my boats.
Quite a hobby of mine. Such a charming
day for a row on the lake. I know you like
boating," he added, as he addressed Lilian.
"And, Mrs. Clarencourt, you'll come too ?"

Mrs. Clarencourt would. It was more
than the Honourable Jim bargained for, he
had quite expected a refusal from the elder
lady ; he had positively heard her say that she
detested aquatic excursions of any kind, and
would far rather remain on *terra firma* than
trust herself in a rickety boat, no matter how
safe it might be. There was nothing left for
it but to stick his glass in his eye and try to
look pleased, which he succeeded in doing to
a great extent, though he felt considerably

put out. With that intent the trio set off together, and they were just strolling down the slope of turf which led to the water's edge when Mrs. Clarencourt addressed Ledsham.

" I know you will excuse me, Mr. Ledsham, but there is Mr. Laxby Randall ; we have not met since my return, and he is such a dear good man. I must ask you to forgive me, but I shall be so delighted if you will take me for a row some other day."

The Honourable Jim was simply delighted. A trump card had suddenly turned up in the person of the rector. He had not hoped for such good luck. It was difficult to him to conceal the pleasure he felt, but he did it very well, looked a trifle glum, requested Mrs. Clarencourt not to apologize to him, he should be only too pleased at any future time, &c. In another moment the widow had slipped her arm through the rector's, and was walking with him back to the gardens, and Lilian was alone with the very man of all others whom she wished to avoid. She saw no way out of her dilemma; she could not possibly ask him to excuse *her* too, it would be rude. There was no alternative, she must face it, so Lilian put her dainty little foot, the bare sight of which caused Jim Ledsham's heart to beat like a sledge-hammer, inside the gondola, and suffered him to place her comfortably on the luxurious cushions. A few skilful strokes of the scull sent the light boat skimming out into the lake, clear of the water lilies which grew close round the margin, the petals and centres of which glistened, snowy white and gold, in the clear bright sunlight. Jim Ledsham relinquished his oar and sat down opposite Lilian, entirely screened from observation by the silk-striped curtains.

"I am awfully glad she did not come ; how kind it was of old Randall to turn up just at the right moment."

Lilian did not venture to ask his reason, it would have given him his cue, and not knowing quite what to say, waited until he should speak again.

"You don't mind smoking ?"

"Not in the least," she answered. Her only thought at that instant was how she should get out of the boat and away from her tormentor. The one striking feature about Ledsham was the color of his eyes, yellowish-grey describes it most accurately, but what was more noticeable about them was that they never seemed still, but restlessly wandered anywhere and everywhere, yet refused to meet your gaze. The rest of his face was handsome, and despite the blemish most men would not have relished him as a rival.

"Miss Fabyn, I am going to ask you a question. Will you promise to answer me?"

"No, I cannot bind myself so rashly."

"Well, I will take my chance. Do you know why I did not want Mrs. Clarencourt to come with us, and why 1 was so glad when Randall appeared?"

Lilian's face flushed scarlet, and then paled as white as the blossom of the long-stemmed lilies through which they drifted, but she bit her pink lips and closed them firmly.

" Whatever might have been your reason I am not so curious as to hazard a guess, Mr. Ledsham. It cannot possibly interest me."

The rebuff did not affect Jim Ledsham much, he was not troubled with a thin skin. He only knew that she looked lovely, and longed to gaze into the liquid depths of her hazel eyes, with his arms round her and her lips to his, and, what was more, he resolved to do it, and was not a man to pause to count the cost. He thought he loved her, and he meant to win her by fair means or foul.

" I will tell you. I wished to see you alone, to have you to myself. Of late you have avoided me ; your manner has changed and grown cold. What I have done to offend you I know not. If I have erred, it has been in loving you too well." He had drawn nearer to her as he spoke, and had deftly slipped his arm round her waist. Lilian struggled but she was power-less in his grasp; passion gleamed in his eyes, and his hot breath fanned her cheek.

" Release me, Mr. Ledsham "—her hazel eyes flashed with contempt as she spoke. " Is this your boasted love, to insult me, weak and defenceless in your grasp ? "

" You *shall* hear me, Lilian. By heaven, I mean no harm! I have dogged your very footsteps, and followed your shadow to pour these words into your ear. Be my wife. Look round; all this will be mine. I have means. I would give the wealth of the Indies, if I had it, to possess you, but I offer you my heart." He was alone with her. He forgot his station and rank as the son of an English peer ; he for-got the respect due to her as a lady and a guest, and pressed his lips again and again to hers. Lilian was pale and trem-bling with nervousness, and loathing of the man.

" Let me go, Mr. Ledsham! Do you call yourself a gentleman? I tell you you are a disgrace to your order. Let me go. I hate you."

"And you refuse my love?"

"Yes, once and for ever."

"Lilian, hear me; you cannot be so cruel as——"

"Pull this boat to the shore, Mr. Ledsham, and permit me to land. I have said all I intend to say upon this subject. I do not love you, and that should be sufficient." She came of a good old stock, and her blood was fired by the disgraceful treatment offered to her.

The Honourable Jim saw that the game was up for the present, but he did not despair altogether. He would be revenged, if nothing else. So he stuck his glass up, and sulkily pulled to the flight of marble steps where they had embarked. "So cursedly proud, and *I asked* her to marry me. 'Not a gentleman, and a disgrace to my order.' She shall have cause to repent having used such language to me," were the thoughts that filled Ledsham's mind, as he walked silently by Lilian's side in the direction of the house, and half an hour afterwards saw her depart with Lady Fabyn for The Towers.

END OF VOL. I.